AF622208

WOLF

WOLF

BY
ALBERT PAYSON TERHUNE

Author of BUFF: A COLLIE,
FUTHER ADVENTURES OF LAD,
TREVE, A DOG NAMED CHIPS, etc

KALPAZ

©Reserved

All rights reserved. No part of this work may be reproduced, stored, adapted, or transmitted in any form or by any means, electronic, mechanical, photocopying, microfilming recording or otherwise, or translated in any language, without the prior written permission of the copyright owner and the publisher. The book is sold subject to the condition that it shall not, by way of trade or otherwise, be lent, resold, hired out, or otherwise circulated without the prior publisher's written consent in any form of binding or cover other than that in which it is published.

The views and opinions expressed in this book are author(s) own and the facts reported by them have been verified to the extent possible, and the publishers are not in any way liable for the same.

ISBN: 978-93-5128-369-0(HB)

First Published in 1925
Indian Reprint in 2017

Published by

Kalpaz Publications
C-30, Satyawati Nagar,
Delhi – 110052
E-mail: kalpaz@hotmail.com
Website: kalpazpublications.com
Ph.: +91-9212142040

Cataloging in Publication Data—DK
Courtesy: D.K. Agencies (P) Ltd. <docinfo@dkagencies.com>

Terhune, Albert Payson, 1872-1942, **author.**
Wolf / by Albert Payson Terhune.
pages cm
"First published in 1925"
ISBN 9789351283690 (HB)

1. Dogs—Juvenile fiction. 2. Children's stories, American.
I. Title.

PZ10.3.T273Wol 2017 DDC 813.4 23

Albert Payson Terhune

Albert Payson Terhune was born on 21st December 1872, in New Jersey, United States. Terhune's father was the Reverend Edward Payson Terhune and his mother, Mary Virginia Hawes, was a writer of household management books and pre-Civil War novels under the name Marion Harland. He was one of six children, having four sisters and one brother, but only two of his sisters survived until adulthood. Further tragedy beset the family when his own wife, Lorraine Bryson Terhune, died four days after giving birth to their only child. He later remarried Anice Terhune, but had no more children.

Terhune received a Bachelor of Arts degree from Columbia University in 1893. The following year, he took a job as a reporter at the New York newspaper *The Evening World*, a position he held for the next twenty years. During this period, he began to publish works of fiction, such as *Dr. Dale: A Story Without A Moral* (1900), *The New Mayor* (1907), *Caleb Conover, Railroader* (1907), and *The Fighter* (1909). However, it was his short stories about his collie Lad, published in *Red Book, Saturday Evening Post, Ladies' Home Journal, Hartford*

Courant, and the *Atlantic Monthly*, that brought him mainstream success. A dozen of these tales were collected in to novel form and released as *Lad: A Dog* in 1919. This was a best-seller and in 1962 was adapted into a feature film. He went on to produce over thirty novels focussing on the lives of dogs and enjoyed much success in the genre.

Terhune's interest in canines was by no means restricted to fiction. He became a celebrated dog-breeder, specialising in rough collies, lines of which still exist in the breed today. Sunnybank kennels were the most famous collie kennels in the United States and the estate is now open to the public and known as Terhune Memorial Park. Terhune died on 18th February 1942 and was buried at the Pompton Reformed Church in Pompton Lakes, New Jersey.

My Book is Dedicated

To the Memory of

WOLF

A GALLANT LITTLE COLLIE AND MY CHUM

CONTENTS

CHAPTER I: HIS OFF-DAY

WOLF

CHAPTER I: HIS OFF-DAY

IT was not Wolf's day. Few days were Wolf's days. Wolf had an inborn gift for ill-luck. Trouble was his birthright. There are such dogs; even as there are such people.

More than once the fiery red-gold collie had the wit and the grit to make Trouble his servant, rather than his tyrant. But not on this day.

There is a fire-blue little lake in the North Jersey hinterland; with soft green hills that encircle it as though they loved it. On its eastern shore, facing the sunset across the water, a point of sloping land runs out;—a point that is a hillside lawn, girdled by gnarled and mighty oak trees, more than two hundred years old.

On a plateau framed in giant oaks, above the Point, is an old rambling vine-clad gray stucco house, red-roofed and trimmed with black-brown timbers. Behind the house and behind the barns which lie in a hollow a hundred yards from it, the oak-grove hillside rises gently again, for a furlong, with the driveway winding through it; until it ends in the stone wall that borders the highroad. Beyond the wall and the road stretch anew the meadows and the woodlands of The Place, with the mountain forests behind them.

Here, with the Mistress and the Master whose chum he was, dwelt Sunnybank Lad; glorious mahogany-and-snow collie, whose eyes had a Soul back of them.

Here Lad lived out his sixteen years of staunch hero-life and of d'Artagnan-like adventure. Here he died, in the fullness of serene old age. Here he sleeps, near the house he loved and guarded.

Some of you have read the tales of Lad's exploits. You may remember his temperamental gold-and-white mate, Lady; and Bruce, the beautiful giant collie without flaw of nature or of physique.

If so you will also recall Wolf, the stormy little son of Lad and Lady. (More of you will remember reading, a year or so ago, in the newspapers, the account of Wolf's hero-death. For nearly every paper in America devoted much space to this shining climax of his tumultuous life.)

Lad went through his eventful long career, serene and loved; his dashing adventures bringing him vast credit and admiration. Bruce the Beautiful lived out a serene tenure of days; petted, praised, happy.

Even Rex, the big crossbreed at the lodge-gate, seldom got into serious trouble;—at least seldom until a blizzard day you may have read of—a day when his murder-battle with old Laddie in the snow-choked forests behind The Place found its ending in a knife-thrust through his insane heart.

With Wolf, in his early years, it was different. He was born to Trouble. And he ran true to form.

Within him throbbed the loyal, staunch, uncannily wise nature of his mighty sire, Lad. But through his veins, too, frisked the temperamental wildness of his mother, Lady.

The two strains did not blend. They warred. Bit by bit, the Lad strain predominated; but only after several years had passed.

For instance, it was the heritage of Laddie's unafraid and chivalrous soul which at the last made Wolf throw his life away gayly and gloriously to save a worthless cur.

But in his early years, the mixture of Lad and Lady in his makeup was as incongruous as the clash of flint and steel. The result often took the form of one hundred per cent bad luck for the strange young dog.

Wolf's ill fortune began when his fuzzily pudgy grayish-yellow puppy body shaped up into something approaching maturity and when the indeterminate fuzz merged into a ruddy gold coat. Collie puppies, up to four months, are adorably pudgy and fluffy and appealing. That is why even the poorest of them find ready purchasers at that stage.

Not until the roundness of body and indeterminate shape of head and foreface set into their permanent lines can the most expert beholder tell with certainty what the young collie is going to develop into.

It was so with Wolf. His sire and dam, each in a wholly different way, were glorious specimens of the highest type of thoroughbred. Their son, Wolf, was as highborn as they. His was the heritage of collie perfection. But he missed this heritage by a mile.

The Mistress and the Master watched with increasing gloom their hopes of a son of Lad and Lady which should combine the best points of both parents. They had bragged happily of breeding a collie that should be a pride to The Place; at dog-shows and at home.

Wolf was not such a collie.

He was undersized; though wirily powerful and as lithe as a panther. His coat, which should have been wavily abundant, was as short and as thick as a chow's. It was not unlike a chow's in texture and growth. His bushy tail was three inches too short. His head was broad where it should have been chiseled into classic lines. His muzzle was not long enough for the rest of his head. The "stop" above it was too prominent. His glowing dark eyes were round; not almond-shaped or slanted as called for in the "Standard of the Breed."

In brief, he was not a true type of collie; though of royally pure lineage. He was a throwback;—a throwback almost to the ancestral wolves which form the trunk and roots of the collie family-tree. It was this queer outward resemblance to a young timber-wolf which gave him his name.

Yet Wolf was beautiful, in his own odd way; and he was surpassingly strong and swift. That broad brain-space of his was vibrant with incipient wisdom.

The fact remained that he was anything but a show-type of collie and that he gave no sign of reflecting future credit on The Place or on his breeders. He would have been sold, in those early days, except that nobody would pay a decent price for such a dog, and because the Mistress—the natural protector of all The Place's weak and luckless Little People—pitied him.

From the first, he gave to the Mistress the absolute loyal devotion which had always been given her by Lad. This devotion did not keep Wolf, in puppyhood, from transgressing The Place's every law and winning for himself a repute for sheer naughtiness which strained all the Mistress's gentle patience.

Yes, he was a trouble-center; seemingly a changeling in disposition and in luck; as well as in body. His elfin cleverness served only to intensify this; and it blurred the traits of steadfastness he had inherited from Lad.

From the beginning, as I have said, he was the adoring, if erratic, slave of the Mistress. He loved the Master, too, in only a lesser degree. For the rest of mankind or womankind he had not the slightest use; to the day of his death. He endured them when he must; and he kept out of their way when he could. He molested no one, so long as people let him alone. But he resented with slashing teeth any effort at familiarity from the world at large. Children were the sole exceptions. Like the Mistress and like Lad, he had an odd sense of protection for anything defenseless.

Yet, there was one of The Place's Little People which Wolf failed to recognize at first glance as belonging to the helpless class. Thereby hangs this story.

It began on a day when a well-meaning friend sent the Mistress a pale-gold canary in an equally pale-gold cage. The Place was a bird-sanctuary. Never a year when at least a score of nests were not built among the heavy wistaria vines that draped the house and the verandas. The big trees of the lakeside lawn were athrill with music. There was bird-melody from gray dawn till dark, in summer and in spring. As sensibly send a bottle of nice clean sand to the Sahara as a tame singing bird to that abode of song.

The undesired gift was made welcome. The gilt cage was hung in the alcove of the dining-room bay window. The canary swung there, and screeched his heart out with gusts of shrill music, in sorry contrast to the myriad liquid notes of songsparrow and thrush and robin and catbird and oriole in the sweet old trees outside.

Wolf found a house door open and strolled interestedly into the dining-room; where, at the Mistress's instructions, the Master was hanging the shiny cage in the alcove arch. The canary hopped feverishly about, chirping in falsetto excitement. The cage, on its gilded spring, swung jerkily up and down in the flare of morning sunlight.

To Wolf, this was a most engaging, if puzzling, sight. Never in his single year of life had he seen a captive bird nor a gorgeous and fascinatingly jiggling cage. He gave vent to his feelings by jumping up and trying to get the scent of this queer new creature at close quarters. For a dog relies most on his sense of smell and least on his eyes. A peculiar sight must be verified by his nostrils.

Wolf's blunt young nose rapped the metal floor of the cage and set it to jiggling tenfold, while the canary squawked loud terror at the impact.

"Down!" commanded the Master, angered at what seemed to him an act of wanton puppyish mischief. "*Down!*"

He enforced his order by a sharp rap of his open knuckles across the collie's hips.

At the word and the blow, Wolf dropped to the floor, almost midway in a second spring. There he stood; in no way cowed, but resentful and wondering. He was still young enough to be bewildered by a myriad prohibitions whose nature and meaning he could not understand. An older dog gets to taking them philosophically for granted.

Apparently, in leaping up to get the scent of that wildly hopping bird, Wolf had broken some complicated law. The Master's single mandate of "Down!" would have sufficed, without the knuckle-rap.

"Leave that cage alone, Wolf," went on the angered voice, speaking incisively now. "Leave it *alone!*"

The dog comprehended. Here was something else that must be avoided; something else that a collie must remember to keep away from. Nevertheless, the memory of the slap rankled. Glumly, Wolf left the room and the house. He knew he was in disgrace. Disgrace cuts into a sensitive dog like a whiplash.

The next noon, Wolf was drowsing on a rug in the raftered living room, midway between the two open porch doors. The day was sultrily hot. Here, close to the floor and between the two doors there was a cool breath of draught. A collie has a genius for finding such spots; when summer heat makes his heavy coat a burden.

The Mistress and the Master and a guest were sitting on the porch, in the few minutes before lunch should be announced. A maid was going to and fro, between dining room and kitchen, arranging the table.

Dogs have certain vast advantages over humans. A human can see farther and more distinctly, except in the dark, than can a dog. But a human cannot hear with half the acuteness or with half the understanding of a dog; while a human's sense of smell is to a dog's as a baby's rattle to a machine gun.

Scent is a dog's surest and strongest sense. It verifies or corrects all his other senses. (That is why a dog is not interested in his own image in the mirror. His nostrils tell him no other dog is facing him there. He believes his nose and therefore discredits his eyes.)

By dint of smell and of hearing, now, Wolf became aware of a new and forbidden presence in the nearby dining room. He knew that the kitchen cat—an ill-favored pinkish brown feline—had slipped into the room, in the wake of the maid; and was hiding there, under the table. This was in the days when long table-cloths were still in vogue; offering cave-like hiding places for such intruders.

The maid went out to the kitchen again, closing the door behind her. Wolf heard the canary chirp loudly in fear.

With a worried interest in a scene whose nature he foresaw, he got up from the rug and strolled into the dining room. He arrived just in time to see a pinky-brown shape leap upward and attach its talon claws to the bottom of the cage.

The flimsy spring broke. Down upon the hardwood floor, with a metallic clash, tumbled the cage. To shield the wildly fluttering canary from the probing claws, Wolf bounded forward; growling sharp menace at the marauder. The cat fled, spitting, as he rushed at her. She took refuge beneath the table with its sheltering cloth.

Under the cloth dived Wolf, in punitive pursuit. The cat twined herself amid the table's tangle of carven central legs, whence the dog sought in vain to dislodge her.

At the same instant, the Mistress and the Master came hurrying in, drawn by the resonant clatter of the fallen cage. The guest—a portly and uninvited neighbor named Glure, whom some of you remember—followed.

There on the floor, amid a halo of spattered birdseed and water, lay the cage; its panic-stricken occupant beating frantically against the bars with frayed yellow wings. There, too, protruding from under the tablecloth, appeared Wolf's tail and a part of one hindleg.

The picture told its own story to the Master and to Glure. The dog had sneaked into the dining-room and, disobeying orders, had knocked down the canary cage. Then, hearing the footsteps of the humans, he had crawled under the table to hide.

Without a word, the Master seized the dog's wolf-brush tail; yanked him forth into the light; pointed to the overturned cage which the Mistress was righting; and slapped the collie heavily across the loins, twice. The punishment was accompanied by a word or so of gruff rebuke which hurt worse than did the blows.

Wolf made no attempt to escape; nor did he cringe. He stood there, mute, sullen, submissive, under the manual and verbal onslaught. He was uncannily wise, this slender young throwback-collie. He knew he was being punished for another's fault; and he knew that this was damnably unjust.

But he was already old enough to know that justice is not an infallible human attribute; and that men are prone to follow temper rather than reason in dealing with dogs. His Master—his god—was striking him. Wherefore the young collie stood mute and statue-like; and took his harsh treatment unflinchingly.

The Place's luncheon guest, Mr. Hamilcar Q. Glure, was thrilled with horror at the canary's mishap. Righteous indignation surged up within him. As the Master drew back from the second blow, Mr. Glure brought his own hamlike right hand down, resoundingly, across Wolf's hips.

In less than a second, Glure was reeling backward across the room, stamping to regain his balance which had been imperilled by the lightning onslaught of a snarling red-gold demon; and he was bellowing loudly for help.

At Glure's alien touch, Wolf had ceased all at once to be proudly submissive to punishment. In a flash he had hurled himself at the throat of his assailant; with the eager intent of severing the fat man's jugular. He missed the throat by a matter of inches, as his victim staggered back; and his razor-teeth slashed at the upflung fat hand which sought to fend him off.

"*Wolf!*" yelled the Master.

At the call, Wolf desisted from his campaign of homicide. Quivering all over, he left the bawling and stamping Glure and faced his owner. There he stood, his big dark eyes fixed on the face of the man who was his god, the man who had power of life and death over him.

The dog had just broken the all-sacred Guest Law. Well he knew that. And well he knew the penalty might be death. Yet, with no effort to escape, he stood waiting for doom to fall.

The Master eyed him for a moment in silence. Then he said, quietly:

"Out!"

The dog dropped head and tail and pattered miserably from the room. He had been ordered away like any worthless puppy. The insult rankled.

"Drop that chair, please, Glure," went on the Master in the same tone, turning to his guest. "He won't go for you again. You're in no danger. I'm sorry he tackled you. But it isn't safe or wise to hit another man's dog. I can't blame him for what he did."

Glure, lowering the chair he had caught up as a weapon, became aware of his own bitten hand—an item the Master had not perceived.

Before the guest could call attention to the hurt, the Mistress spoke. She had been setting down the cage when Wolf had flown at Glure.

"I called to you not to strike him, dear," she said, to her husband. "You didn't hear me. Wolf didn't deserve punishing. It wasn't he who upset the cage."

"It wasn't, eh?" demanded the Master. "Nobody else could have done it. How do you know it wasn't?"

"Because I know Wolf," was the confident answer. "Yesterday you told him to leave the cage alone. It isn't like him to—"

"It isn't like him to go sneaking under the table, either," countered the Master. "He never showed a streak of cowardice before. But that's what he did when he heard us coming in."

"I think not," she contradicted. "Yes, I know he was going under the table when we saw him. But he wasn't hiding. I believe he had some more honest reason for going there. Wait a minute."

Kneeling, she lifted the white cloth that hung low over the table-side. There, revealed, was the pink-brown kitchen cat, cowering amid the central legs in a praiseworthy quest for privacy. The storm of warfare, outside, in the room had reduced her to moveless terror. To one half-sheathed claw was sticking the single yellow feather she had been able to impale in her futile grabs for the bird.

The sight told its own story. The Mistress looked from the scared cat to the Master. He did not meet her eye. She said nothing. Nor was there triumph or even reproach in her look. Nothing but sorrow.

That was the Mistress's way. Without scolding or scowling or "disciplining," she always managed to convey her meaning. Wherefore, folk loved her; and sought to win her approval.

"You're right," said the Master, briefly. "It was rotten of me."

"Pshaw!" scoffed Glure, having assured himself that the cuff of his tweed coat had protected his hand from more than a graze from the slashing teeth. "Pshaw, man! What if it *was* the cat and not the cur? One licking, more or less, doesn't matter to a dog."

"One injustice, more or less, matters," said the Master, self-disgustedly. "I struck him and scolded him for something he didn't do. I'm—I'm going out to look for him."

"If it comes to that," observed Glure, sourly, "he ought to have been licked within an inch of his life for pitching into *me*, the way he did."

The Master's mouth flew ajar. A red hot reply sizzled in his throat. But it died unspoken; for the Mistress was saying:

"Yes, please go and find him. You can make him understand it was a mistake. Please do."

Glure snorted in high derision. The Master ignored the grossly offensive sound; and went forth on his quest of the collie.

But Wolf was not in the house nor on the veranda nor in hail of the calling voice.

Perhaps it is ancestral sub-memory that sends an unhappy collie to the woods for consolation. Even as sick collies creep to the woods to die. To the woods Wolf had gone now, in his despondency. Loping across the rolling lawns he gained the lakeside meadow at The Place's far end; and thence plunged into the cool green of the forest.

Here were giant oaks which had been giant oaks when ill-clad Continental militiamen camped in their shade a hundred-and-forty-odd-years ago. Here too were thickets of witch hazel and witch-elm and spicy sassafrass clumps. Here, alas! were the barkless gray-white ghosts of a thousand big chestnut trees slain by the Blight.

Here, as well, were windfallen trunks, more or less decayed, where partridge and woodpecker drummed and where pitying Nature had flung a pall of soft trailing vines above the tree-corpses. Here were mysterious trails and holes and warrens. Here were a myriad scents fascinatingly perceptible to a collie, though too subtle for human nostrils to note.

Above all brooded the mystic hot hush of early mid-summer afternoon. (Underfoot, of course, varying the lush loveliness of fern and moss and partridge-vine, were strewn occasional crumpled newspapers and greasy wooden dishes and picked chicken bones and other evidences of picnic desecration of God's silent wilderness.)

To-day, Wolf took no heed of alluring smells nor of the scurry of rabbit nor the whirr of pheasant. His heart with sick within him. Not for the first time was he learning that life is bigger than are those who must live it. In disgrace with his deities and smarting under blows and black injustice, he ran on; without objective; flitting through the shadows with the furtive sidewise gait of a timber-wolf.

Then, suddenly, he halted in his run. His unguided feet had brought him near the highroad. Only a single fringe of trees separated him from it. And there, he was brought up, standing, by the sound of sobs.

Sitting disconsolately against a tree-trunk, not fifty feet ahead of him, was a child.

Two families from Montclair had gone picnicking, that day, in their two cars. The little girl of one family had wandered into the woods, picking wildflowers, after the rest had finished their roadside lunch. One of the cars started homeward ahead of the other. The child's parents supposed their daughter had gone in this, as sometimes she did. They had set off without her.

When she returned to the road with her armful of blossoms, she found herself deserted. Starting back into the woods in an illogical hope that her father might perhaps be looking for her there, she realized suddenly that she was lost. And she sat down to cry. Here Wolf found her.

Forgetting his own sulks, in the spectacle of a child's grief, the collie trotted up to the youngster; wagging his tail in friendly greeting. He licked her wet cheeks with his pink tongue and patted at her lap with one white forepaw.

The child looked up gratefully from her crying fit, glad of such company in this desolate place. She threw both arms around Wolf's furry neck, in a strangling hug. Then she bade him shake hands. To her delight he obeyed.

Before she realized it, she had forgotten she was deserted; and she was reveling in a romp with this charming new acquaintance. She threw sticks for the dog to retrieve. She made him "speak" for a bit of cake she found in her pocket. She even taught him to play a primitive sort of hide-and-seek with her, among the big tree-trunks. Then, urged on by the zest of exploration and wholly without fear, now that she had found so valiant an escort, she set forth on a woodland ramble with him.

For half an hour or more, the two wandered in happy aimlessness, through the fragrant warm woods. It was a wonderful exploring trip for them both. In the joy of it, Wolf forgot his grievances and his sulks.

Then, as they chanced to stroll near the highroad again, a big yellow-and-black butterfly fluttered up from a clump of wild azaleas just ahead of them. The child cried out in delight, and gave chase. The butterfly flitted languidly out across the road, the child close behind. She was blind and deaf to everything except the pursuit.

Wolf was not interested in butterflies. He trotted along at the little girl's side, but with no thrill of the hunt. This, until she pattered out into the road. Then, all at once, he was on the alert.

He knew the menace of the open road for dogs and for humans alike, in this juggernaut-era of fast-driven motor cars. On that very curve, not a month earlier, a heedless puppy had been killed in scampering across.

Unseen, beyond the trees which marked the bend, a motor car was whirring. The collie heard and smelt it. Then he saw its goggled beetle-nose thrust itself swiftly around the curve.

With a bound, Wolf caught up with the running child. He overtook her in mid-road. Here was no time for gentleness nor persuasion. Seizing the hem of her white dress, he tugged with all his wiry strength, pulling her backward and almost off her tired feet.

The car sped past, not six inches from where he had dragged her to the road-edge; the driver slamming on his brakes and shouting foolishly.

The first of the two picnic cars had had engine trouble ten miles down the line. The second car had caught up with it. The child's parents discovered in horror that their daughter was not aboard the other car.

Fearing she might have wandered far into the woods or even have fallen into the lake, they made their way back at lawless speed in search of her.

Spinning around a bend, the father caught sight of his lost youngster directly in front of him. She was at the roadside, in the teeth-grip of a vicious dog which had seized her by the skirt and seemed to be pulling her into the bushes to devour her.

Handbrake and footbrake stripped the gears. The car skidded to a bumpy stop. Before it had fairly halted, the father was overside. As he went, he caught up the heavy crank.

Straight for Wolf he rushed, crank aloft. The dog saw him coming; and loosed his grip on the child's skirt, springing in front of her, to guard her from this new danger.

But, even as he sprang, he heard her cry in joy: "Daddy! *Daddy!*" And he knew this man was menacing him and not her.

The crank whistled through the air in a skull-crushing blow for the dog's head. But the dog was not there. With ridiculous ease, Wolf eluded the clumsy weapon. The crank hit the asphalt road with a force that snapped its flawed steel and numbed its wielder's arm to the shoulder.

As the man groped for one of the broken pieces with his left arm, Wolf snarled low and in utter loathing; then wheeled about and with insulting deliberation trotted down the road, homeward.

He had seen a woman clamber hastily and tearfully out of the car; and catch the child in her arms. His little new-found chum had been reclaimed by her own people. Wolf's guardianship was ended. Incidentally, one of those people of hers had made an industrious effort to kill him. Humans were strange creatures.

Along the road edge trotted Wolf. The Place's gates were not a furlong beyond. Toward them he made his way; his deceptively fast wolf-trot eating up the distance quickly, for all his seeming deliberation.

Only once did he check his stride; and then but for an instant. The Mistress and the Master were standing in the gateway; whither they had strolled, after Glure's departure, in order to plan for some new gate-pier vines.

But, immediately, the dog resumed his advance. He had sinned. He had attacked a sacred guest. Furthermore, he was believed to have broken the law by knocking down that miserable canary cage. Dire penalties might well be in store for him.

Yet unafraid he went to meet such penalties. These two people were his gods. Already his sulks were forgotten. He saw the two whom he worshiped. He ran forward happily to meet them; whatever that meeting might entail.

Close behind him chugged a fast-driven motor car. From that car was issuing a furious voice. The child had been gathered aboard. Her father, deaf to her incoherent protests, was seeking to run down the vicious dog that had attacked his darling offspring.

Wolf trotted straight up to the Mistress.

"Why, Wolfie!" she exclaimed. "Where have you been, all this time?"

"That your dog?" boomed a voice from an abruptly halted car.

From the front seat descended the little girl's father; clutching again the larger portion of the broken crank.

"Yes," said the Master, eyeing the red-faced sire as he stamped up to them. "What about it?"

"What about it, hey?" stormed the father. "Well, he bit my poor little girl. *That's* 'what about it!' Bit her terribly. Tried to drag her into the woods and kill her. He—"

"Wolf never harmed a child, in all his life!" declared the Mistress. "He is—"

"Didn't, hey?" boomed the father. "Well, I saw him. So did my wife. We'll swear to it. Frightened her half to death and tried to tear her throat out. She's scared into convulsions, pretty near. She—"

His bellow changed to a gobble; and he stared with eyes a-bulge.

Wriggling out of her mother's hold, the weeping child had gotten to the ground. Now, rushing over to Wolf, she flung her plump arms about his neck and laid her cheek against his furry face.

"You shan't hurt him!" she sobbed passionately. "You *shan't*, Daddy! He found me when I was all lost. And we had a darling time. He—"

"Huh?" grunted the flabbergasted man, mouth agape.

"And then I was going across the road and I didn't see the car till it was right on top of me; and he pulled me back, so it couldn't hit me. And then you tried to kill him and then you chased him. And you're not going to kill him, Daddy! *You're not going to!* I kept trying to tell you, all the time you chased him. And you kept bellowing so loud you wouldn't hear me. You're not going to kill him, a *bit*. Nobody is. He's —"

Her torrent of words fought in vain to rise above the convulsive sobs that were shaking her. She gave over further attempt at clear speech; but continued to hug Wolf's head to her breast and to glare defiantly through her tears, at her flabbergasted sire.

The Mistress knelt beside the little girl, petting her and crooning:

"Nobody's going to hurt him, dear. And you're right. He's a brave, *brave* dog. Now, suppose you let me take him down to the house and give him his dinner? Shan't I? He looks hungry."

The child quitted her tight hold. Still crying, she kissed the dog on the tiny white spot on top of his head. Then, face averted, she hurried back to her mother in the car. Her father stood irresolute and breathing hard; the broken crank dangling from his hand.

"Your motor is still running," observed the Master. "Don't you think it'd be wise to get the good of your gas by letting it take you home?"

Turning, he followed his wife and Wolf down the drive-way. Wolf was walking close beside the Mistress, his woes and perplexities and grievances quite forgotten under the touch of her hand and the soft voice that was telling him what a splendid little dog he was. At sound of the Master's step, he looked back at him, grinning and with tail awag.

"If I had a third foot," mused the Master, "I'd kick myself with it. It's bad enough to be unjust to a fellow-man. But it's worse to treat a dog as I treated Wolf. Because I can't explain to him or apologize or anything. He—"

"Don't worry," counseled the Mistress. "See, he's forgiven you already. When God put dogs into this unjust world of ours, He gave them power of divine forgiveness; to make up to them for all the injustice they were going to receive. Sometimes I think perhaps that puts dogs just a little bit above us humans. Or perhaps it doesn't. . . . How about it, Wolf?"

CHAPTER II: HIS FRIENDS

CHAPTER II: HIS FRIENDS

UP from the lakeside woods trotted Wolf. He moved with an affectedly mincing gait and he carried his head a little on one side. For he knew he was doing something clever and that a group of people on The Place's veranda were admiring it.

Vain, with all the calmly colossal vanity of a collie, the wiry little dog got scant enough meed of praise, in those first years of his life. And the occasional drops of it which seeped through to him from time to time made him inordinately proud.

The Place's two great dogs—magnificent old Sunnybank Lad and the beautiful Bruce—were chronic centers of admiration. For the mischievous and eccentric young Wolf there was little of this.

True, when Wolf saw a litter of two-month-old puppies playing on the driveway, while a recklessly-driven delivery truck bore down upon them, he won lavish approval by dashing off the porch, rounding them up with the skill of a veteran sheep-herder, and hustling them to the safety of the driveside ditch. For this queer atavistic exploit, the Mistress had petted him and told him he was a splendid dog. Her laudation had gone to his head.

Henceforth, not only did he round up and drive to safety all pups that ventured into the road; but he went further and shoved out of the way any of the grown dogs or other animals that happened to stroll across the drive when a car was in sight. Always at such times he would glance eagerly at the Mistress for praise. Always the praise was forthcoming.

But, for the most part, Wolf went uncheered by human admiration. An exception came when, of his own accord, he galloped to the woodland pasture one day and rounded up and drove to the stable The Place's two big work-horses, Sintram and Lass.

This he had done on seeing two of the men drag the farm-wagon out from the shed. It was a sample of true reasoning power. The superintendent had told of it; and Wolf had been petted for his odd feat of mentality.

But even then, scolding followed swift on the heels of praise.

A human child gets a laugh by some unintentionally clever speech; and then makes a pest of himself for the rest of the day by trying to say other funny things. It was so with Wolf.

Having been praised for bringing the work-horses up from the pasture at a time when they chanced to be needed, he fell into the way of bringing them thence six or seven times a day; until the frenzied protest of the superintendent and a stern rebuke from the Master led him to see that the stunt had lost its popularity. Since when he did it only on order.

Even thus, he drew further admiration; this time through no cleverness of his own.

A horse, as a rule, becomes idiotically attached to any dog with whom it is brought into close association. Seldom does a dog reciprocate this affection, except in the mildest way and as a deserved tribute to his own charms. But the devotion of the horse for his canine pal is unbounded.

Perhaps from his bossily authoritative way of rounding them up, the first time, perhaps from recognition of his half-human brain, both Sintram and Lass were Wolf's adoring friends.

When he ran condescendingly along in front of the farm-wagon they reduced the driver to blasphemy by trying to keep up with him; and then by bolting in pursuit whenever he rounded a corner, out of their sight. Similarly, when he lagged behind the wagon, they would not move faster than at a crawl; and were forever looking back to locate their chum.

The new way whereby he drew human attention was by going to the pasture, loping along in front of the two grazing horses and then trotting unconcernedly back to the stable. Immediately, both horses followed; close at his heels. Whatever deviation from a straight line he might make, on this stableward trip, they followed slavishly.

It was pretty to see the little collie strut pompously toward the stable in a circuitous route, with the two huge horses following, in loving obedience, a step or two behind him.

To-day the Master had ordained that the horses be brought up from the pasture and shut in the stable a hundred yards behind the house. The Mistress, on her morning walk, had noted that the May flies were torturing them cruelly, down in the dense woods; and she thought they would be more comfortable in their breezy stalls.

She and the Master were about to start on a motor drive, with two guests. For the amusement of these guests, she sent Wolf after the horses.

Fully aware of his position in the center of the stage, Wolf obeyed eagerly the command. At first sight of him, as he trotted in front of them, in the depths of the woods, Sintram and Lass lifted their heads from browsing among the tender bush-leaves, and wheeled about to follow him.

Mincingly, with his head on one side and his dark eyes half-shut, Wolf turned toward the house; the big horses following, in docile worship of their dog-friend. Thus far, all went well. But Wolf was never content to leave well enough alone. A glorious idea came to him.

The way to the stable led well beyond the rear of the house. It occurred to Wolf that he could make the trip far more spectacular and win for himself more praise from the watching humans, if he should guide his charges across the lawn at the house's front; and thence around by a wide detour to the stables. In such way, the procession would be well in sight from the veranda where the Mistress and the Master and the two guests were standing.

Accordingly, as he left the orchard, he did not keep straight ahead; but bore widely to the left; and toward the house-front.

Along came Wolf, trotting pridefully, his gold-red coat ashine, his white paws prancing. Close behind, ambled the two horses. Reaching the wide heliotrope bed which was the Mistress's joy, Wolf cleared it at a bound; as he had been taught to. The horses did not. Plodding heavily, their two sets of four great shod hoofs stamped over the soft loam border, grinding the fragrant heliotrope blossoms and plants deep into the soil; uprooting or otherwise destroying beautiful flowers by the hundred.

"Yes," the Master was saying to one of the guests, "people have been at me to give up the two horses and buy a tractor, instead. But a tractor won't whinny at you when you go into the barn in the morning; and a—"

He was interrupted by an exclamation from the Mistress; who observed for the first time the erratic course the parade was taking. Gayly led by Wolf, the faithful steeds had traversed the heliotrope border and were now treading broadly along a line of exquisite white Madonna lilies. As the Mistress called out in unhappy dismay, Wolf's circuitous course led his two followers through a bed of many-hued pansies and thence over a clump of young rose trees.

Attila's havoc rush through Europe, a few centuries ago, did far less damage, per square inch.

"Wolf!" yelled the Master.

Instantly, at the fierce summons, Wolf forsook his charges and galloped up to the veranda. His gay conceit was gone. From the Master's tone he realized that somehow he was in disgrace once more; though for no reason that he could grasp.

But the sharp command admitted of no delay. Wherefore he made for the veranda at top speed; leaping clean over a crescent row of new-blooming scarlet phlox.

Honestly and ponderously the two giant horses followed this direction taken by their guide; quickening their gait to a lumbering canter as they tore destructively through the phlox and across the circle of veranda lawn. The turf was soft from a recent rain; and their iron shoes left pretty sliding marks on it.

"He was just showing off, dear," expostulated the Mistress, as her husband strode toward the crestfallenly advancing collie. "He didn't mean any harm. Here, Wolf!" she broke off, pointing in the direction of the stables. "Herd them there. Go!"

In a flash, the dog had wheeled back to the oncoming horses; swinging them about, to their patient astonishment, and driving them before him at a gallop, toward the barn. He could not understand, even yet, why his triumphal march had failed to receive its usual laudation and why he had been ordered in disgrace to complete his drover task.

Life was like that. Daily, there seemed more and more ideas the puzzled young dog could not grasp; more and more complications to this game of existence.

One of the men met the horses in the barnyard and drove them to their box-stalls; shutting them in. Wolf, tail adroop, went back to the veranda.

It did not occur to him to keep out of the way of the two humans he loved; until their wrath should have cooled. They were his gods. He wanted to be near them, whether they approved of him just then, or not. And this is the way of a collie.

He found the Mistress mourning the demolition of her beloved plants. The Master pointed to the scene of destruction; and, in a sizzling mouthful of words, scolded the dog for the mischief he had caused. To be rebuked was shame enough. But to have it done in the presence of strangers seared Wolf's over-sensitive self-esteem to the raw. Gloomily he went into the house and lay down; head between paws; crushed of spirit.

But he came back to interest in life, half an hour later, when the car was brought up to the door. The Mistress and the Master and the two guests got aboard. So did Lad and Bruce. Wolf pattered expectantly forth to attach himself to the party. He was fanatical in his craze for motoring.

"Want to come along, Wolfie?" asked the Mistress. "There's plenty of room."

The dog needed no second bidding. He understood the invitation as fully as though he were human. Indeed, much association with humans had taught him to read voices unerringly and to grasp the meanings of many simple words and phrases.

In delight he danced down the steps and to the car. Then, abruptly, he stopped in his tracks. For, from the front seat, the Master was saying:

"No! You can't go, Wolf. You've been in mischief again and you've spoiled flowers that are worth twice as much as you are. You'll stay at home. It'll be a lesson to you."

The collie looked up at him in mute appeal; then turned to the Mistress. In his heart he knew she would not veto the Master's decree; for these two worked as one in dealing with their dogs, and in all other details of life. It was thus they kept calm discipline among the Little People of The Place. But the pity, now, in the Mistress's face gave him a shred of hope.

It was not until the car had been in motion for some moments that the Mistress spoke.

"Wolf really meant no harm," she said. "He was only trying to amuse us, by bringing the horses past the front door. Wouldn't the scolding have been punishment enough?"

"No," growled the Master. "It wouldn't. He's forever starting trouble. He needs some kind of punishment that'll sink in. He'll remember this."

"You said one very wise thing," enthused a soulful guest, on the rear seat, "when you told him he had destroyed flowers worth twice as much as he is. When an ugly dog spoils anything so richly beautiful and rare as a flower—"

"I said a very *silly* thing," contradicted the Master, crankily. "And it was a lie, too. The left hindleg of any dog on The Place—even Wolf—is worth more than all the flowers that ever grew, since the Garden of Eden was planted."

The soulful guest gasped aloud at such sacrilege. But the Master did not heed her prattled protests. He was sorry he had treated the collie as he had. Cooling down, he realized the gay impulse which had led Wolf to plan that gala procession past the house.

Long association with such super-dogs as Lad and Bruce had not fitted his temper to deal with a harum-scarum-like Wolf. He was unduly impatient with the wild-spirited youngster.

(Years later, when regret could do no good, the Master was to stand above a pathetically still red-gold body—the body of a hero dog whose prowess and gallant death were recorded at much length in every newspaper in America,—and was to wish from the depths of a sore heart that he had dealt differently with that same collie in the tumultuous early days;—in the days before he and Wolf had grown to understand and esteem each other. As usual the foolishly futile wish came too late to benefit anyone.)

Wolf, meanwhile, left alone and in redoubled disgrace, went back into the house and lay down in front of the living room's empty fireplace.

Here in winter evenings he was wont to lie, shoulder to shoulder with Lad and Bruce, cuddled close to the Mistress's feet, and blinking in drowsy comfort into the blaze; while the wind roared outside and the snow scratched hungrily at the window-panes.

Even in hot weather, this was his favorite resting-place; just as the "cave" under the adjoining music room's piano was Lad's and as the bearskin rug outside the Master's study was Bruce's.

There lay Wolf; profoundly miserable at the ill treatment piled on him. At last he dozed.

Through his dreams filtered an idea that winter had come back. For though there was no cheery heat from the hearth, yet to his sensitive nostrils came the reek of smoke.

Presently, he woke, and glanced at the hearth and then around the room. No fire twinkled and snapped on the andirons. Nor was there haze in the room. Nevertheless, faintly and from far off, still came that recurrent whiff of smoke.

Lazily, he got up, stretched himself fore and aft in true collie fashion, and strolled forth to investigate. Not that smoke carried any sinister message to him; but he was temperamentally curious; and he remembered furthermore that no fewer than three gorgeously chaseable rats had scuttled forth from a brush fire a month earlier.

The Place's superintendent and two laborers were at work with scythes in the sixteen-acre pasture, across the road, a quarter-mile from the house, on the far slopes of a hill. The maids were in the village at the movies that afternoon. Lad and Bruce had gone on the motor-jaunt. Wolf was alone on the home-tract of The Place.

One of the two laborers had eaten his lunch in the barn loft. Then, the meal finished, he had made certain the superintendent was nowhere in view and had leaned back luxuriously in the hay for an after-lunch smoke. At the superintendent's call from below he had knocked out his supposedly extinct pipe and had come down to work.

For the past three hours the tiny red coal from the bottom of the pipe had been doing more vigorous work than any of the laborers. The growing area of sparks and embers had begotten a tongue of flame. The rest was destruction.

Wolf sallied forth from the house to behold a solid mass of yellow fire belching from the square door of the hayloft and to see the flames creeping snakelike downward along the outside of the stable walls.

Here was a highly diverting spectacle. The dog paused to give it his full and interested attention. Head on one side and ears cocked, he surveyed the holocaust. He had ever an eye for the unusual. This was one of the most unusual sights in his two short years of life. He sat down, wolf-like, on his haunches, to enjoy it at his ease.

Then, on a sudden, he was on his feet again; his wiry body vibrant, the condescending air of interest merged in dire excitement.

For, from somewhere inside that blazing building came to him a sound which nobody who once has heard it can readily forget.

It was the raucous screech of a panic-stricken horse.

Again the eerie sound keened forth above the crackle and roar of the flames. And with it now came the noise of vainly hammering hoofs.

His two friends. The two big, gentle work-horses that followed him

Wolf went into action. In no time he was at the barn and had darted in through the stable door. The smoke here was not so strangling as in the loft; but it was thick enough to make all things wellnigh invisible; and to choke the on-rushing dog and sting his tender nostrils to torture.

His first impulse was to get out of this painful and blinding and smothering place and into the clean air. But the stable was as rackety now as it was unbearable. Both horses were screaming and were plunging madly to and fro in their box stalls. An eddy of breeze cleared the upper spaces of the stable, ever so little, for an instant. Through the lifted smoke Wolf had a glimpse of vague gigantic figures rearing high and dashing themselves against the sides of the stalls. Sparks glowed in their manes. New showers of sparks fell in stinging profusion on their glossy coats. The loft-flooring above them was wellnigh burned through. From its widening cracks, snakes of fire were swooping downward at the frantic prisoners.

This was Wolf's first experience with fire as an enemy. Hitherto it had been a warming and pretty thing, pleasant to look at blinkingly. Now he saw it not as a slave to mortals but in its true light as an unleashed devil.

It was menacing these two big friends of his;—these horses which were so queerly helpless to get away from it and whose gentle calm had turned to a crazy terror.

Wolf knew well how to open the doors of the box stalls from the outside. The old-fashioned latches needed only a single downward pressure of a paw, to slip up and let the oaken doors swing open.

There was a Colonial latch somewhat like it on one of the house doors. As a trick, the Mistress long since had taught Wolf to open this; even as hundreds of collies have been taught.

It was ridiculously easy. Wolf had been proud of the accomplishment and had exercised it by opening that house door, in season and out of season, a hundred times; until he had been forbidden to tamper with it again. Later, discovering the box stall doors had the same general sort of latch he had amused himself by opening them.

By chance, he had never been seen doing this; though thrice the horses had gotten out of their stalls and into the vegetable garden and the cornfield in some mysterious way; and much oftener the superintendent had called the other workers to account for their apparent neglect to fasten the doors shut when they put the horses into the stalls.

Wolf tucked down his head and made for the door of the nearest stall. Suffocating, burned, in keen pain, he found the latch. Standing on his hindlegs he slapped it smartly with one cinder-grimed paw. The door swung wide. By that time Wolf was at the second stall's door and patting its latch in like fashion.

Having opened both doors he considered his share in the performance was at an end. Every moment in that hell of fire and smoke was torment to him. Having released his two equine friends, he sped out of the stable and into the open. There, he sucked in great lungfuls of clean air and rolled on the ground to stifle the hornet-like sparks that stuck to his red-gold coat.

Presently, he paused in this comforting occupation and stared wonderingly at the flaming barn. The stall doors were open. So was the stable door. Yet neither of the horses had emerged from the building.

Wolf could not understand. The horses continued to kick and plunge and scream as before; only now with an added intensity and agony; as the heat and smoke waxed more intolerable and as the spark-showers from above changed to a steady downpour.

It seemed to the collie the simplest thing imaginable to run out of such a place; once the way were made clear as he had made it. Yet the horses were still in there. It did not make sense.

With all his uncanny young wisdom, Wolf did not know—nor does the average human—that a horse is the most cowardly and most stupid creature of its size on the face of the earth. An alley cat or a mongrel cur or a mangy donkey or a halfgrown mule—any of these have thrice the brain and four times the reasoning powers of the average horse.

Your horse will shy in fright from a bit of paper lying in the road. He will shy at the same piece of paper in the same place in the road a dozen days in succession.

Your horse will let any stranger get on his back and ride him away; despite his lifelong master's most alluring calls to him to come back.

Your horse, in face of fire, is as senseless as a year-old baby. To lead him from a burning building, one must swathe his head in a coat to keep him from running back into the blaze.

Your horse, being noble of aspect and keeping his mouth shut, goes through life with a reputation for lofty wisdom (as does many a human for like cause). He is a fool. Poets have raved of his mental and soul greatness;—poets most of whom never broke or owned or rode a horse. And mankind at large has taken the poets' word for it.

So now, Sintram and Lass were quite insane with terror. The doors of their stalls gaped wide. So did the stable door; pointing clearly the way to safety. But the horror of the flames had stolen what little brains the poor brutes possessed. Up and down their prisonless prisons they tore, helpless to escape; though the loft floor above them was sagging perilously now; ready at any instant to let down a mountain of blazing hay and boards upon them to roast them alive.

Back into the barn dashed Wolf, perhaps with some new inkling of his two friends' stark stupidity.

Sintram's stall was nearest the door. Into it whirled Wolf; seeking to drive out its occupant. But Sintram was too far gone in terror to heed guidance. Wolf saw that, almost at once. Harsher measures were necessary.

In a leap, the collie had seized the frantic brute by the nose, dodging by some miracle the flailing forefeet. With a jerk Wolf slung himself sidewise. The anguish of the bitten nostril made Sintram veer with him. Around twisted the dog, his hindlegs braced on the hot floor, now that he had pulled the roaring Sintram down on all fours. And, under that tormenting pressure, the horse swung around once more with him.

Suddenly, Wolf loosed his nose-grip and spun back to Sintram's heels. A vicious bite in the left hock made the horse lunge forward, out of the stall and into the space behind it; the space leading to the wide open outer door.

By the time he had cleared the stall, Wolf was out of it, too, and tackling the screaming Lass in the adjoining box.

Here the same tactics prevailed; though with more difficulty and at the expense of a bloody shoulder-graze from the mare's panic-driven hoof.

Out into the open space Lass was propelled by a deep bite in the flank. There, she and her mate jostled confusedly and in utter impotence; stung by sparks and flame and choked with black smoke reek that blinded them.

Wolf himself was in scarce better case. His coat was singed. His eyes were running and throbbed with pain. He could not breathe. His shoulder was grievously hurt from the kick-graze. A million points of agony marked the drift of the spark torrent on his head and back.

But apparently this was no time to die or even to try to escape. There was work on hand. Having probed to the utmost the brainlessness of these captive horses, he knew he must do their thinking for them, if he or they were to get out alive.

Ignoring his own torture, he sprang into the welter of flying hoofs and plunging bodies.

Yet he worked, as ever, with a set purpose; in spite of the seeming wildness of his attack. A well-calculated nip here, a slash there; clever distance-judging and direction-gauging under the seemingly maniac show of ferocity. The one way to get those creatures out of the hell-trap was to make them more afraid of him than of the fire. This was Wolf's job. This he proceeded to do.

Everywhere at once he tore into the frenzied horses; biting, slashing, driving; turning, heading off. It was a beautiful bit of herdsmanship; this tag game with death. Through his ever increasing pain, Wolf's gay mischief spirit flared forth. He was doing grand work. Also he was having the time of his life.

It was all a question of a second or two; there in the swirl of furnace heat. Then, out into the open lumbered the insane horses; a lightning flash of red-gold at their heels, at their flanks, at their underbodies.

Outside the barn they veered and swung about; the aspect of the blazing stables drawing them almost irresistibly; as it has drawn thousands of their kind in like crises.

But Wolf would not have it so.

Foreseeing their impulse to gallop back into the inferno, he was at them again in redoubled fury; not so much as waiting to draw breath into his tormented lungs or to clear his eyes of sparks and wetness and smoke.

Like a tiger he was ravening at their swaying heads. Biting, snarling, fighting demoniacally, he instilled once more into their dense brains a fear of himself that was greater than the panic-lure of the fire.

Snorting, neighing, they whirled around. And Wolf—a ruddy thunderbolt—was after them. Giving them no chance to pause or to turn, he harried them ferociously from behind; driving them in headlong flight away from the barn.

At their first step, the loft floor crashed in; heaping a fiery avalanche into the stalls and rear-space where they had been plunging.

Onward Wolf sent them flying. They fled from his murderous onslaught as from a demon. Now, the runaway impulse had seized them; and it was wellnigh as strong as had been the attraction of the flames. Down the lawn they thundered blindly and thence down the steep bank into the lake; halting only when they were shoulder-deep in water. There they slithered to a stop and stared dully about them; their brains clearing. They were too worn out nervously to go farther; too apathetic to do more than stand there and snort and to let the cool lake water ease the pang of their myriad smarting burns.

A man had rounded the top of the hill and had broken into a run.

He was the laborer whose pipe-coal had started the conflagration. Sent back to the barn for a scythe, to replace a broken one, he caught sight of the fire and hastened toward it. As he ran he saw the horses splash into the lake, Wolf driving them fiercely.

Two minutes later he was back in the mowing field, bellowing loudly to the superintendent:

"The barn's afire! I got the two horses out, all right, all right. But it was touch-and-go. Hurry up!"

Wolf saw the horses come to a halt deep in the water; and he knew their madness had fallen from them. His work was done. No danger that the team would traverse that distance, now, for the sake of re-entering the burning stable. Wolf could call it a day and rest.

With a grunt of relief, he trotted into the lake and lay down. The water came up to his ears. Its icy caress was rapture to him. The cool of it salved his burns and braced his racked nerves. He lay there and lapped it down his parched throat. He breathed deep; clearing the smarting smoke from his anguished lungs.

Casting a languid eye toward the distant blaze he saw the three mowers making for it at full speed, dragging The Place's chemical engine behind them. From the lake, too, several fishermen were landing; to give aid.

Well, it was no business of Wolf's. He had done his part. His friends, the horses, were safe. He could afford to wallow here in the wet coolness and take his ease. There was no other animal in the barn to be herded to safety.

After a while, instinct told him of something better than mere water for the easing of burns. He got up and followed the shore-line to a springy spot where the bank merged into an inviting patch of mud. To this he went; and in it he rolled; its healing powers taking the smart from his hurts.

An hour later the chug of a familiar motor came to his ears. Gayly he jumped up from his muddy bed and made for the house. He had wrought gloriously, this day, had Wolf. And he longed for the Mistress's dear praise.

The car was coming to a stop at the front door when Wolf ranged alongside. At sight of his mudcaked coat, the flower-loving guest cried out in disgust and hugged closer to her the white skirt she wore.

"Oh, do take him away!" she begged.

"Clear out, Wolf!" ordered the Master. "Isn't one bit of mischief a day enough for you? I can't see how any single dog can get into so many kinds of senseless trouble. Clear out!"

The collie slunk away. The rebuke in the Master's tone and the guest's look of contempt were hard to bear. He felt very tired and very sick. Surely it had not been wrong of him to play hide-and-seek with death, in an attempt to save the two horses that loved him! Then why was he in disgrace, again?

Up from the half-destroyed, half-extinguished barn hurried a knot of smoke-smeared men, the superintendent at their head. The fire was out; though the upper half of the stables was a wreck. The chemical engine and tons of lake-water had enabled the toilers to stop the conflagration before the barn was a total loss. Now, seeing the car, they ran up to tell the news to The Place's two owners.

Out of the babel of talk, presently, boomed the voice of the day laborer who had discovered the blaze.

"I got the horses out, Boss!" he declaimed. "Risked my life to do it. I had a tussle to make 'em go. But I drove 'em to the lake and left 'em there. I'd 'a' done it easier, only Wolf kep' gettin' in my way. He —"

"He would," commented the Master. "That's the best thing Wolf does;—getting in the way."

"Say!" spoke up one of the fishermen who had been gazing open-mouthed at the laborer. "There's a lie out, and a good big one. I saw the fire and I rowed for the shore here. About every stroke or two I turned my head to look. One of the times I turned, I saw a collie dog come pirooting out of the barn driving two horses ahead of him. They tried to run back; the way horses will. But he kept after 'em, till he drove 'em clean into the lake, right near where I was landing. Just then I saw this chap come running down the hill toward the barn. It was the dog that—"

"That's right!" spoke up a man from another boat. "My brother was rowing. I was in the stern and I saw the whole thing. That dog is a wonder."

The laborer edged modestly out of sight around the house; his hopes of largesse and of fame collapsing.

The Mistress also disappeared from the group. The Master found her, a few minutes later; Wolf's dirty body held close to her white sport suit as she sat with one arm about the dog, crooning softly to him and petting his mud-smeared head.

It was three days later that the Master sent Wolf to the woodland pasture once more, to show off for another guest, by leading the two horses back to the stable. Eager to do his popular trick, the collie bounded along on his mission. He found Sintram and Lass grazing in the lush grass at the edge of the woods.

At sight and scent of him, the two horses remembered all at once his murderous assault and the merciless slashes and nips he had used in goading them forth from the barn.

With common impulse they flung up their heads and fled in fright from him, snorting and trembling.

Sadly, wonderingly, the little collie gazed after them. Then he realized what had happened.

He had lost his adoring big friends;—had lost them forever. Henceforth they were to look on him as a dread enemy and persecutor. No more would they follow gladly where he led; nor so much as suffer him to come near them. Love had changed to cringing fear; friendship to horror.

Head and tail adroop, Wolf trotted back to the house.

He avoided the Mistress's eye, as he lay down in a furry and unhappy ball at her feet. But she stooped and petted him and told him he was a wonderful little dog. And under her praise and petting, Wolf grew almost happy again.

He had lost the friendship of two silly horses. But the Mistress understood. The Mistress always understood.

CHAPTER III: TRAPPED!

CHAPTER III: TRAPPED!

A MAN named Glowdy rented a cottage and a few acres of land; a quarter mile or so from The Place.

To this cottage in the early spring he brought his family and a large and nondescript shorthaired brindled dog. The man called his huge dog "Fluffy;" having given him this pet name the day he bought him —a downy and pudgy two-month-old pup—from a street vendor, one Christmas week.

Now the collies at The Place had scant association with the isolated neighborhood's few other dogs. Lad and Bruce were patricians—snobs, if you will—who looked down coldly upon non-Sunnybank canines. Even Rex, the big crossbreed at the gate lodge, did not deign to pick outside acquaintances.

But Wolf was different. Wolf was rankly democratic—a rare trait in a collie. True, with all humans save only the Mistress and the Master, he was icily, even fiercely, aloof. But with every stray dog he met in the course of his rambles, he was wont to pick up an immediate friendship. Seeing him trot chummily along the road with such an one, the Mistress used to say in mock vexation:

"Wolfie's gone slumming again!"

But with no other neighborhood dog did Wolf form such instant and complete chumship as with the gigantic misnamed Fluffy.

He and Fluffy had chanced to meet, during a woodland run; a few days after Glowdy moved into the cottage near the lake. At once, the two became bosom friends. Day after day, Wolf would trot consequentially over to the Glowdy cottage, to meet and frisk with his dear new chum and to wander off in quest of rabbits or squirrels in the deep woods back of the road.

In like fashion, Fluffy would visit The Place, sometimes—in search of Wolf. But his aspect at such visits was not consequential and unafraid, as was Wolf's. Instead, the big brindle would slink furtively into sight, around some outbuilding.

If Wolf chanced to catch his scent or to see him, well and good. But if, instead, Lad or the stately Bruce were in view. Fluffy was greeted by a haughtily disgusted growl and a show of eyeteeth. Snarling, he would fade out of sight in that curiously furtive manner of his.

For Lad, to the day of his death, was an opponent few dogs would have cared to clash with. Nor was Bruce, with all his melancholy gentleness, a much less formidable guardian of The Place.

"I wish that mongrel brute of Glowdy's would keep away from here!" declared the Master as he and the Mistress, on a tour of the rose-garden, saw Fluffy's brindly bulk slink into sight amid the lakeside shrubbery. "He's a cur. He won't look any human in the face. I know the type. A wealth of mean cunning and treachery and a born distrust of all humans. If I didn't want to keep out of neighborhood rows, I'd write Glowdy to keep him at home; and I'd load a cartridge with salt to scare the cur away. He—"

The Master broke off with a grunt of contempt. Wolf, who had been walking placidly at the Mistress's side, frisked forward in happy welcome, toward the big mongrel; touching noses with him and wagging his tail and wriggling his muscular gold-red body in warmest greeting.

"See there!" said the Master, pointing to the two. "That's Wolf, all over. Lad and Bruce turn up their noses at the cur. But Wolf hails him as a loved comrade. He's a mongrel, himself, at heart."

"He is not!" contradicted the Mistress, eagerly. "Wolf is as pure thoroughbred at heart as he is in ancestry. He likes to slum. That's all. He's like some wellbred boy who has yearnings to go and play with gutter children. Wolf is more like a normal boy than like a dog, anyway. Come back, Wolfie!"

At her call, Wolf left off welcoming his disreputable friend and came cantering back to her.

"See!" she declared, as she petted the collie's upthrust head. "He'd ever so much rather be with us than with Fluffy. Wolfie, aren't you ashamed to know such down-at-heel, sneaky dogs as that? Aren't you?"

The mongrel had vanished, at the advance of the two humans.

"I think I'll hint to the constable, over in the village, that Glowdy's dog may be the one the reward is out for," continued the Master, glancing sourly through the shrubbery for trace of the mongrel. "He —"

"What reward?" asked the Mistress.

"Didn't you see it, on the post office bulletin board? The Grange has offered a fifty dollar reward for the unknown dog that's been killing chickens, wholesale, from Oakland to Paterson; for the past month. He's destroyed something like a hundred fowls, Strake told me. A regular 'Killer.' He has a positive genius for it. Some dogs have, you know. Only a few of them; but enough of them to make legislatures pass the stringent anti-dog laws that are so unjust to decent dogs. Sometimes they go after sheep; sometimes after fowls. And they do it so trickily that they're almost never caught. I hear the Grange offer is going to be increased to $100. If it is, in these times of shut-down mills, there'll be a hundred out-of-work men spending their nights gunning for the Killer."

"But why in the world do you say Mr. Glowdy's dog may be the one?" inquired the Mistress. "You've no reason for thinking so, have you?"

"No," admitted the Master, "I haven't. Except that he looks like the kind of dog that would enjoy doing anything criminal. As a matter of fact, one of the men tells me Glowdy keeps Fluffy shut up in his barn, every night;—'for fear he'll be stolen.' As if even a blind kleptomaniac would steal a mutt like that! And since all the killings are done at night, I suppose that's a cast-iron alibi for Fluffy. The real Killer may live ten miles from here. I'm glad we've stopped keeping chickens."

Ten feet away, lying flat against the ground, in the thickest of the shrubbery, Fluffy could hear and see them; just as Wolf could scent the hidden dog. Fluffy heard his own name spoken, repeatedly, by the two humans; and with no loving intonation. His lips curled back from his huge yellowish teeth; and the look in his small eyes was not friendly. As the Mistress and the Master sauntered on, beyond him, the mongrel made his way homeward.

The Master had no gift for logic or for intuition. Yet, for once he chanced to have hit upon the truth; in his belief that the big brindle was the Killer for which the Grange reward was offered.

Fluffy had been bred and reared in the city. Only during the past few months had he known anything of the country life that is a dog's true heritage. Some blend in his mixed ancestry made him revel in this new life and understand by instinct the mysteries of forest running and of trailing and the furtiveness of the wild.

During one of his lone rambles across a field, he had chanced to see a strayed chicken. A wild ancestral impulse surged up in him. As a rule when a dog chases and kills a fowl the racket is heard for a half-mile. A fox and a wolf and a coyote slay silently. So it was with Fluffy.

A stomach-to-earth stalking whose stealth was instinctive;—a lightning-swift and dextrous swoop;—and the chicken was dead without so much as a squawk. The dog did not eat his prey. He was not hungry. He had slain for sport, not for meat. And the thrill of the slaughter was the most overpowering emotion he had ever known.

It was something which must be done again; something which must not be prevented by human interference. His innate craft warned him not to repeat the deed where he could be seen by prying menfolk.

He knew, by nature, that night was the safest time for that sort of hunting. It was at night that his cousins, the foxes and wolves and coyotes, fared forth to the kill.

But, at night, Glowdy always shut the mongrel in the dismantled little barn back of the cottage; lest he be stolen.

That same evening Fluffy solved the problem of escape.

Getting up from the gunnysack mat on the barn floor, he made a tour of his sleeping quarters. A barrel stood just beneath a paneless window. On this the dog mounted. With inherent craft he abstained from jumping out, until a cautious look through the opening showed him a wagon-body tiptilted against the exterior wall, a foot or two away. Up this incline and thence by an easy jump in through the window;—it was a simple exploit for any active animal.

Having arranged for both exit and ingress, Fluffy sallied out upon a night of adventure. Early next morning, Glowdy found him drowsing on the gunnysack mat in the barn. Early next morning a farmer a mile away found eleven of his best chickens dead and mangled in an unlocked henhouse.

Thus the depredations began.

Late on the evening after the meeting in the rose garden, Wolf made his usual before-bedtime round of The Place, in true watchdog fashion; before settling down to his nightily snooze on the porth. As he passed along, just inside the low stone wall which skirted the highway, he heard the stealthy pad-pad-pad of feet on the road outside. By sound and by scent he recognized his dear friend, Fluffy. At a bound he was over the wall and touching noses with the brindle.

Often as he and Fluffy had been together in the daytime, this happened to be their first meeting at night. Wolf was delighted that the tedium of his all-night vigil as watchdog was to be relieved by the presence of a chum.

But Fluffy was not minded to turn aside from his chosen program for the mere sake of romping on The Place's lawns with Wolf or for accompanying him on a run through the woods in pursuit of elusive rabbits. Chickens were much easier and more alluring prey.

Having touched noses civilly with his adoring chum, the mongrel continued his loping progress. Wolf stared at him, in wonder at such curt treatment. Then apparently making up his mind that only some adventure of enthralling interest could account for Fluffy's haste, he galloped after him, to share it.

It was the first time and the last in Wolf's ten years of life that he deserted his self-appointed task of night-watchman for The Place. But he was only a little more than three years old; and his responsibilities still weighed upon him fitfully and lightly.

Wherefore, swept on by curiosity and by a wish to be party to whatever exploit the mongrel might be planning, he ranged alongside the loping Fluffy and ran shoulder to shoulder with him.

Thus, for nearly a mile, they went on through the darkness. At last, Fluffy turned aside from the main road and into a lane which led to a farmhouse;—a farmhouse he had not visited for so long that its owners might reasonably have been lulled to security from invasion.

Nearing the house, the brindle made a silent detour of it and approached softly the henhouse behind the stables.

Now all this was Greek to Wolf. But the young collie inferred by the queer new excitement in his chum's manner that something exhilaratingly worthwhile was in store. Hence, in unconscious mimicry, he crouched as the other crouched, halted when he halted, and crept forward when he crept forward. It made no sense to Wolf; but he was enjoying it; even as he always enjoyed anything savoring of the dramatic or of a game.

The henhouse door was shut; but its wooden window was invitingly open; a large window which hung from a hinge at its top and which was kept open by a stick propped at one edge of it.

With the lithe ease of a cat, the mongrel leaped upward and through the aperture; coming to ground noiselessly inside the henhouse. On the low perch just above Fluffy's head were huddled four scrawny old fowls; the coop's only occupants.

Wolf hesitated not an instant in following. Gathering himself for the easy jump, he too landed in the henhouse, at Fluffy's side. He looked about him. Surely, here was nothing interesting; nothing to account for his chum's zestful eagerness to come hither, nor for the hysteric chatter of the mongrel's huge jaws as he peered upward at the fowls.

Wolf glanced inquiringly at Fluffy; but the brindle was too tight-gripped in his slaughter-mania to heed the smaller dog. Trembling, with jaws a-chatter, he was surveying the perched chickens, making his choice as to the victim for his first assault.

Wolf yawned, and lay down to watch. He was only mildly interested now in his chum's unprecedented manner. In the chickens Wolf was not at all interested. Chickens were no novelty to him. He had seen chickens a thousand times. Noisy, uninspiring, squawky creatures, they were; with a passion of running across roads in front of The Place's cars. Surely, there was nothing about a mere chicken to cause all this tense excitement of Fluffy's.

An instant later, the mongrel made his choice of a victim. Noiselessly, deftly, he sprang upward; his jaws meeting in the neck of a barnyard rooster of great age and toughness. As he sprang he was vaguely aware of some cobweblike barrier which his upflung body brushed through.

As his teeth gripped skillfully the rooster's neck, two right impossible things happened. They happened, almost simultaneously.

There was a blinding glare of white light that filled the whole coop and set the chickens to fluttering groundward. At nearly the same time there was a dull slamming sound; as the rusty-hinged wooden window sagged shut.

The mongrel wasted not the fraction of a second. Like a coyote in similar straits, he acted on instinct; by bolting for safety.

Scarce had the grip on the rooster been succeeded by that dazzling flare, before Fluffy had dropped his prey and in practically the same motion had sprung for the window-opening. So incredibly swift was he that he actually smote against the falling shutter before its latch could click fast.

The push knocked wide the closing slab of wood. With a scramble and a heave, a bunch of hair from his back remaining in the latch, he was out of the trap. The shutter, released, fell again; and its latch locked tight.

But in the ever-so-brief interim, Wolf, too, had gone into action.

The flash had brought him to his feet. The fleeing brindle had collided with him as both faced the window. Fearing lest Wolf's effort to escape might impede his own progress and block the narrow opening, Fluffy snapped viciously sidewise at the collie. The snap did not delay for an instant the speed of the mongrel's departure. But it ripped Wolf's left ear and seared his cheek.

Incidentally, it brought the collie to an abrupt halt. For a moment he stood blinking toward the suddenly closed shutter, past which the mongrel had already won his way to safety. Wolf could not understand. He was dazed. The unexplainable flare of light and the slam of the wooden window-shutter were as nothing, by way of surprise, to this vile behavior on the part of his loved chum.

The mongrel had not only jostled him aside but had actually bitten him; and then had gone away and left him trapped;—had attacked and then deserted him! His pal had done this; the big dog that Wolf had been proud to tag around after! He had won safety for himself and he had barred his collie chum from it! Worse—he had wantonly torn the smaller dog's face and ear.

Gradually, the daze faded from Wolf's dark eyes; to be replaced by a deepening smoulder of righteous rage. The fiery little collie's temper was never sound asleep. Now it was fanned to flaming wakefulness. Nor was this a mere gust of vexation. It went clean to the very bottom of a stout heart that never before had known real hate.

His chum had betrayed him; had snapped murderously at him. That was not on the free list. The chum was a chum no more, but a mortal enemy. A collie does not forget nor forgive such things.

Wolf growled, far down in his furry throat. His lips curled back from his white fangs. He took a truculent step toward the locked door of the coop, in pursuit of the traitorous mongrel. Then came the scent of humans and the sound of running feet.

The henhouse door was flung open, from outside. In the threshold stood a sketchily attired man with tousled head and bare feet. He grasped a gun. Behind him were running two other men. One of them waved a flashlight.

A sweeping ray of the electric torch lit up the interior of the hencoop; revealing Wolf who stood blinking in its glare. The gun-bearer whipped his weapon to his shoulder and fired.

But the sweeping light had passed on, as he pulled trigger. Also, Wolf was in motion again; making a dive for the doorway. As a result, the load of buckshot inflicted spectacular damage on the rear wall of the henhouse and clipped the comb off an elderly hen. But not a pellet came within two inches of the escaping Wolf.

Out of the trap fled the collie. Yet he was not in flight from these noisy humans. He was in quest of the mongrel that had betrayed him. To the three men he gave no thought, except that they must not be allowed to detain him. The flame of wholesome rage and punitive hatred was hot in the dog's heart.

The sweeping flashlight revealed him, momentarily, to the trio. The gun-bearer wheeled and fired again in the general direction of the galloping red-gold collie. This time, though the man shot at a venture, he had better luck. For one buckshot ploughed a shallow furrow along the dog's side, stinging him to increased fury. He turned half around and snarled menacingly back at the marksman. Then he continued his fierce run.

He did not feel any special resentment toward these humans. Humans were always doing the wrong thing, anyhow. He added the burning swale of pain along his side to the debt of punishment due the brindle. But for Fluffy he never would have been trapped or shot at. Growling under his breath, his teeth clicking wrathfully, Wolf galloped on through the black night.

A mile or so of sweeping gallop brought him to The Place. He did not pause; nor so much as think of his self-imposed duties as night-watchman. On he swept, past the low stone wall and past the gates. He was in the middle of the highroad. A belated car shot past. Wolf scarce deigned to give it right of way, in his furious run.

Presently he had reached the Glowdy cottage. Now he was running with his nose to the ground. As he ran he caught the scent he sought. It was a fresh scent; not two minutes old.

This way Fluffy had come, in headlong homeward flight. Wolf struck his trail; hackles abristle and lip upcurled. Past the sleeping cottage he ran; and to the small barn far to the rear. Nor did he check his pace until he stood beneath the window through which Fluffy had just bounded. The trail ran up the side of a slanted wagon-body. Hither Wolf followed it. There was no need to sniff further. From the interior of the barn, through the paneless window, came the reek of the mongrel. Through it, too, came a low snarl.

Dogs can read sounds and scents as no human can hope to. Fluffy, newly couched on his gunnysack mat on the barn floor, had heard the oncoming pad of Wolf's feet. He had scented the blood on the collie. He read menace to himself in the ferocious advance. And he answered it by snarling.

The brindle knew by instinct what to expect. He knew what he had done to turn friendship into black enmity. And if he had a sense of humor it was tickled by the new animosity on the part of this younger and slighter dog that had been his fond admirer.

In no wise averse to thrashing so easy a victim, now that the latter had declared war, the big dog came forward to meet his adversary halfway. Or such was his intent.

He mounted the barrel and gathered himself for a spring through the window. But, in through the opening, like a furry gold-red catapult, whizzed the compact body of Wolf. In he flew just as Fluffy had launched himself for his own outward leap. As a result, Wolf collided hard with him in mid-air.

The impact sent both dogs heavily to the wooden floor, several feet below; the brindle underneath.

Landing flat on his back with much pain and more shock, the mongrel's surly temper burst bonds, rendering him insane with murderous fury. That the lesser dog should so have upset and hurt him, in his own home, was a humiliation to be wiped out as swiftly and as violently as might be.

At once Fluffy scrambled to his feet. He was upright again, within a fraction of a second of the time that Wolf had found his own catlike balance. But that fraction of a second sufficed for Wolf to slash venomously at the unprotected underbody of his rising foe.

Maddened afresh, the mongrel hurled himself at the smaller dog, with all his weight and mighty force. The onslaught left no doubt as to his intentions.

But, somehow, Wolf was not there to receive the brunt of the charge nor the punishment of the great ravening jaws.

A fighting collie is not like any other type of fighting dog. He inherits the brain, though not the treacherously savage heart of his wolf-ancestors. He is here and there and everywhere and nowhere; ever biting and slashing, ever ready to shift his hold for a better one. He is not a pleasant opponent.

As the mongrel rushed, Wolf slipped lithely to the left, diving in and slashing as he went. The brindle hurtled above him; the jar knocking the collie down, but doing him no further damage. One of Wolf's keen eyeteeth scored a deep gash in his foe's flank; as he rolled over. Gathering his feet under him in falling, Wolf was up almost as soon as he was down. He was up; and he was flashing in at the mongrel's throat, as the baffled Fluffy whirled to meet him.

Wolf's jaws closed on the brindle's wide studded collar, instead of on the jugular. Seeing his mistake, the collie released the futile hold (which a bulldog would have clung to, perhaps, till death) and easily dodged a new attack from his adversary.

Four times the brindle charged. Four times Wolf eluded his rush. Four times a bite or a slash from the collie served as counter to the mongrel's barren assault. Fluffy might as well have been assailing a hornet. Instinct told Wolf he was no match for this giant in stand-up fight; and that he must rely on speed and brain for the victory.

Then, under the force of much exertion and the smart of his wounds, the mongrel's senses cleared of their blind fury. Back to his aid came the sinister craftiness that was his birthright. And he began to use his brain.

There was no sense in trying to crush to death this wily and elusive youngster. Here in the open space in the barn's center there was too much chance for footwork. Only by cornering Wolf and rendering his speed useless could Fluffy hope to win the battle and kill his ferocious little enemy.

Wherefore, instead of charging again, the brindle turned tail and ran.

Ordinarily, this would have seemed to Wolf a signal that the battle was over; and he would have let his beaten antagonist depart in peace. But his blood was up; and the punitive fury beat hot and hotter in his brain. The brindle could not treat him as he had done, and then hope to get away with a few superficial hurts.

Wolf tore after the retreating mongrel in deadly pursuit.

Fluffy had plunged between two high packing boxes and into the square yard or so of space behind them, in an angle of the barn wall. He knew his ground. Here, more than once, he had penned and killed helpless cats.

Wolf, ignorant of the ruse, flashed in between the boxes at full speed, close upon the heels of his foe. And here, with no space for maneuvering or for retreat, the brindle wheeled about and grappled him.

Instantly, Wolf was aware of his own blunder and of its probably fatal results to himself. There was still chance to back out; and to get away, with only a certain amount of injury. But the little dog was not of a mind to back out. From the day of his birth to the day of his death, he did not know the meaning of fear. He inherited the flame-white courage of his sire, Lad.

He was caught in a newer and far deadlier trap than before. But he did not flinch. He met the brindle's deadly charge, jaw to jaw, foot to foot. True, he was flung prone, under it; and his shoulder was well-nigh broken by the snap of the giant jaws. But he drove his own formidable teeth deep into Fluffy's chest; rending and tearing savagely as he fell.

Down crashed Wolf, buried under the weight of the brute that ravened above him. Holding down the smaller dog by planting his splayed forepaws on the squirming body, the brindle prepared to tear his throat out at leisure. The slaughter time was come. Fluffy was ready to enjoy it to the full.

But a collie down is never a collie beaten. Twisting over on his back, Wolf drew his feet up under him and drove them with all his might upward against the mongrel's slashed stomach. He did this just as Fluffy's jaws had buried themselves in the mattress armor of fur beneath Wolf's throat. The sudden whalebone pressure tore free the brindle's grip, leaving him with a mouthful of hair between his jaws and with practically nothing else to show for his broken hold.

As Fluffy ejected the mass of torn hair from his mouth, preparatory to a fresh dive at his prostrate foe, Wolf took swift advantage of the instant's leeway. Making no effort to get to his feet in that contracted space, he struck upward with the speed and accuracy of a python. His teeth found their coveted mark, during the moment while Fluffy was freeing his own mouth of the fur gag.

Wolf struck for the throat; and he gripped it—this time a half inch above the protecting studded collar. His savage ancestry told him to strike there and to hold on.

The huge mongrel realized belatedly his own dire peril. Rearing, he shook himself with all his brute power. Wolf's slighter body swayed like a limp dishrag, under the force of that shaking. His bullet-grazed side was thumped agonizingly against walls and boxes. But he held on; oblivious of pain and of breath-expelling bang against the surrounding obstacles.

Deeper and deeper he ground those keen white teeth of his. More and more furiously the mongrel lashed about the confined space, tearing at such parts of Wolf's swaying body as he could reach and smiting him anew against the boxes and walls.

Wolf's breath was gone. He was battered and in anguish. But he held on; and he bit deeper. He knew well it was his only hope. Once let the mongrel get free of him and his own last chance would be gone.

A man came hurrying into the barn, carrying a lantern. It was Glowdy, roused from sleep by the din.

The mongrel redoubled his efforts to cripple Wolf into releasing his throat hold. Glowdy came running across the floor toward the battle corner. Above his head he brandished a fat blackthorn walking stick, its knobbed head held clubwise.

Then, all at once, the mongrel's shakings merged into a violent shudder. He sank heavily to the floor; his jugular severed.

Wolf staggered weakly to his feet. Glowdy was rushing at him, stick upraised, bellowing threats. Down came the cudgel with skull-cracking force. But the blow missed Wolf; and the stout stick split in four pieces against the corner of one of the boxes.

Wolf, with a last effort of speed, ran past the shouting man, to the open barn door; and melted foxlike into the darkness.

Early in the morning, as was her custom, the Mistress came out on the veranda, a rose-basket on her arm; to gather flowers for the downstairs rooms. On the doormat lay a truly fearsome object. A second glance was needed to identify this rumpled and bloody and hideously disreputable thing as the wellgroomed Wolf.

At sight of his deity, the collie got stiffly and painfully to his feet, wagging his bushy tail in glad morning welcome. The Mistress dropped her rose-basket and bent solicitously over him.

"Why, Wolfie!" she exclaimed. "What has happened to you? You poor puppy! You're half dead. Wait till I can get some warm water and some—"

Around the side of the house clumped a right warlike figure. At sight of the disheveled collie, it halted dramatically.

"Good morning, Mr. Glowdy," said the Mistress. "If you're looking for my husband—"

"I am!" asserted Glowdy, his voice thick with wrath. "I'd have come over, last night; late as it was. But I was afraid your wild-beast dogs might tackle me, in the dark. I've come to tell you people that this collie of yours broke into my barn, last night, and killed my poor

Fluffy. I caught him at it. I'm here to ask if you'll make me go to law or if you'll settle equitably by paying me Fluffy's full cash value and by shooting this dog. He—"

The Master came out on the veranda in time to hear the speech. Annoyed by the man's domineering tone toward the Mistress, he said:

"I'm afraid we can't pay you Fluffy's full cash value; until Uncle Sam coins something smaller than a cent. As for his killing your dog—that brindle is twice Wolf's size. He—"

Another newcomer came around the house from the driveway. The Place was having a wholesale influx of early morning visitors, today. The second arrival was a college boy, in khaki; and wearing a portentous frown. The frown deepened as his gaze fell on Wolf.

"Hello, Mark!" hailed the Master. "Are you just up or just going to bed? If you want me to go fishing again to-day—"

"I've come on a rather rotten errand," said the boy, bowing embarrassedly to the mistress, and then turning back to her husband. "We've caught the Killer;—the dog that's been looting the henroosts and all that."

"Caught him?" repeated the Master. "Good! How?"

"Dad and I rigged up a string just under the roosts," said the boy, with growing embarrassment. "One end of it was fastened to the prop that held open the window. The other end was connected with a flash-flare; and the big camera was set up in one corner of the coop. We only kept one or two of the oldest fowls in there; as a bait; and we left the door shut and the window open. Last night—the fourth night after we set it—the Killer got in. When he jumped up for the roost, he hit the string. We heard the racket and came out. The dog got away. Our hired man took a shot or two at him, but he missed. Dad is busy in the dark room, now, developing the camera plate. I—I came on, ahead."

"Clever work!" applauded the Master. "Even for a crack photographer like your father. If—"

"I said I came here on a rotten errand," went on the boy. "I came to tell you that Dad and our man and myself all recognized the dog, before he escaped. I wanted to give you the tip, so you can get rid of him, before the Grange finds out and brings suit. Of course none of us is going to tell. But next time he may be caught at his work, by someone who *will* tell. The dog was Wolf."

He stopped abruptly, catching sight for the first time of Glowdy, who had been hidden from him by the veranda post.

"Wolf!" cried the Mistress, incredulously. "Why, that's absurd! We used to keep chickens. Wolf never so much as looked at them. Besides —"

"The Killer, hey?" commented Glowdy. "And then he kills my poor dog, too! I'm thinking there'll be a tidy damage bill for you to settle before you're done. And I see no reason for keeping my mouth shut about it, even if this young fellow does. The courts will make you shoot the dog; besides making you pay all damages and costs. I'm—"

Around the house came still a third visitor; an elderly man, walking in much haste and carrying something at arm's length.

"Good morning!" he greeted the group; then: "Mark, I hurried after you as fast as I could. I suppose you've blurted it all out, before I could get here. I told you it would be better to wait till the plate was developed. Look!"

He held out for inspection an unmounted photographic print, still damp.

The photograph depicted with gratifying clearness the interior of a hencoop. On the roost squatted several half-awakened fowls. In midair, his jaws just closing on the throat of a rooster, hung the big brindle mongrel, Fluffy; caught by the camera at the acme of his leap.

On the coop floor, placid and uninterested, lay Wolf; his aspect mild and assuredly not that of a killer. In fact the camera had caught him in the middle of a yawn.

It was a picture that told its own story, far more vividly than all the words in the language could have done. For a space the five stared mutely at it, while Wolf eyed them inquiringly. The collie had a keen sense for the dramatic. He could feel the general amazement; and he thrilled with curiosity as to its cause. The Mistress was the first to recover the power of speech.

"I'm so sorry, Mr. Glowdy!" she said, softly. "So very, *very* sorry! I think I can promise none of us will say anything about this; and I am sure I can promise the plate and the print will be destroyed. . . . Won't —won't all of you come in and have some breakfast?"

But Glowdy, after gaping blankly at her for a second, gave a wordless grunt and stumped away.

"Wolf," said the Master, bending over the collie and petting the happily upraised head, "I don't suppose any of us will ever guess at just what happened last night. But, whatever it was, I'm the debtor of the man who invented flashlight photography. And so are you, old friend. It's saved you from being shot. Not that I'd have let them shoot you."

The Mistress reappeared with a bowl of warm water and some soft cloths.

"I think I can guess pretty closely at the whole thing," she said, as she began gently to wash the dog's numerous hurts. "But I didn't need the picture, to prove to me that he wasn't the Killer. I knew it."

"How did you know?" queried the boy. "All the evidence—"

"All the evidence I needed," she said, decisively, "was Wolf. Wolf is—Wolf. He couldn't do a mean or underhand thing, if he tried to. Could you, Wolfie?"

Wolf, at sound of his name and of the affectionate tone, wagged his tail, thumpingly, on the veranda floor; and his expressive face took on a look of utterly foolish vanity.

He knew he was being praised for something. He had not the remotest idea what he had done to merit praise in that night of mischief and slaughter. But it was enough that the Mistress was mightily well pleased with him. Nothing else mattered.

CHAPTER IV: THE KIDNAPERS

CHAPTER IV: THE KIDNAPERS

SUNNYBANK Lad—super-collie behind whose sorrowful dark eyes shone a soul—was very very old. His clean athletic lines were blurred by flesh. His swirling gallop had changed by imperceptible degrees to a heavy walk. His acute hearing was dulled.

But the splendid mahogany-and-white coat was as luxuriant as ever. His uncannily clever brain was undimmed. The fearless spirit blazed as strong as in youth. In spite of all this he was growing feebler, month by month. And he slept a great deal.

When the Mistress or the Master set forth for a walk or for a tour of The Place, Lad was as eager as ever to go along. He held jealously to his olden functions as watchdog and chum. But his gait was slow and he tired easily. His trumpeting bark was a hollow ghost of its former resonance.

From earliest days he had been wont to catch the sound of The Place's car, nearly a mile away, at such times as he did not chance to be aboard it; and he had bounded up the long hillside driveway and out into the highroad to meet its return. Never had he mistaken the hum of that particular car for any other. There are many collies with this odd gift.

Now, when he heard the approach of the car, he would get heavily to his feet from his "cave" under the piano or from his corner of the veranda; and walk wearily toward it. But by reason of growing deafness and of slow motion, he no longer met it a quarter mile from home and escorted it gayly in through the gateway and down the drive to the house; there to stand in vibrant welcome on the porch to greet his homecoming deities. He was lucky if he could get fifty feet from the door before the machine reached him.

The Mistress noted his chagrin at not being able, as of old, to escort it to the porch and greet its occupants as they stopped at the front door. Wherefore, she used to slow the motor down to a crawl as she came alongside the dog; and she proceeded at that snail-speed until she came to the stopping place at the porch's center.

Thus Laddie found to his delight that he could still escort her thither, as formerly; and be waiting to welcome her as she descended to the veranda steps. He did not realize that she was retarding the car's speed to let him do this. Day after day she did it on her return from such rides as Lad had not chanced to go on. Which was like the Mistress and which made the old dog very happy by restoring some of his vanishing self-esteem.

To Laddie's fiery little son, Wolf, this daily game of car-creeping had no point at all. Wolf's red gold-and-white body had the speed and sinew of a deer's. Yes and his brain, inherited from his great sire, could guide him amid the thickest and fastest traffic. The motor-swarming highroad had no perils for him.

When the returning car would start down the winding drive Wolf was always on his feet and tensely alert. Not to meet the machine and escort it houseward, as did his sire, but to thrust out of the way any possible puppy or other of the Little People of The Place; and to herd them to safety from the motor's approach.

Wolf had taught himself this wise herding-trick. The Mistress had praised him extravagantly, the first time he did it. That was enough to make it a lifelong habit for the adoring young collie. Ever he would turn expectantly toward her after completing the driveway-police exploit. And always the meed of praise was forthcoming.

Then on a day in 1918—last year of Laddie's long life—the car came down the drive from a trip to the station. The tonneau was full of express parcels and boxes. That was why no dog had been allowed to go with the Mistress and the Master on this short ride.

Lad woke from his drowse under a porch hammock, as the motor drew near. The Mistress was driving. Lad had slept soundly. The deafer of his failing ears had been uppermost. He had not heard the car until it was almost at the house. Guiltily he scrambled to his feet and ran to meet it. But the haste was too much for his unwieldy body's balance.

As he ran down the steps he stumbled; plunging forward and falling directly in front of the automobile.

The Mistress put on the brakes with a vehemence that stripped the gears. She swerved, at the same time, into a tree. But the double precaution was too late to check or to deflect far enough the front wheels.

Wolf appeared, from nowhere in particular; as was Wolf's way. He flashed into view, almost under the car, traveling at whirlwind speed. Straight against his fallen sire he crashed.

Gripping Lad by the shoulder and throwing all his own weight and impetus into the effort, he shoved the larger collie clear of the wheels and a full eighteen inches to one side of the nearer of them.

It was a bit of work so rapid that the eye could scare follow it. The oncoming front wheels missed Lad, clean. One of them grazed Wolf's side, whirling him halfway around but doing him no worse harm.

Wolf trotted back toward the machine. Tail gayly awag; mouth grinning widely, head on one side and eyes closed to shining slits, he came mincing back for his meed of praise from the Mistress.

It had been a pretty and a risky exploit. He had performed it brilliantly. Wolf knew that; just as Wolf always knew when he had done something clever. And he wanted to be told all about it by the Mistress. Her praise had ever been his chief delight in life.

White-faced at the narrowness of her loved old collie's escape from mutilation, the Mistress leaned out to thank Wolf and to tell him what a splendid little dog he was. But before she could speak, Laddie intervened.

All his sixteen-year life, Lad had been acknowledged king of The Place's acres and of its Little People; ruling with stern benevolence and giving loyal worship to his two gods, the Mistress and the Master. Of recent months his growing feebleness had filled his supersensitive old heart with a dull resentment; and had made him crochety in his dealings with the Little People. More and more he stood on his dignity with them.

It was humiliating enough, now, to have fallen down so clumsily and in the Mistress's sight; without being set upon and tossed aside ignominiously by a lesser dog. That was unforgivable.

Not in the least did dazed old Laddie realize that his son had just saved his life. To him the onset had seemed an uncalled-for bit of mischief;—a practical joke that could have no excuse.

Into Lad's brain flamed hot indignation, banishing for the moment his weakness and heavy lassitude. In an instant he was on his feet again —the absurdly small white feet which age and weight had begun to splay. He sprang up as lithely as a cat. In practically the same motion he darted at the unsuspecting Wolf.

The younger dog, with his back turned to his sire, was mincing up to the Mistress, grinning and altogether self-pleased. A furry thunder-bolt smote him from behind; bowling him clean over, by dint of vast weight. A pair of pitifully useless old jaws were ravening at his throat.

For a moment, Wolf writhed, helpless, under that impact; pinned down by a bulk and a strength too great for him; his fur-armored throat at the mercy of the fierce jaws that tugged at it.

But Lad's brief flash of power faded. The unnatural force ebbed from him. Wolf slithered, catlike, from under the pinioning weight and regained his footing. Then he wheeled to do battle.

It was not safe for anything or anybody on earth, save only the Mistress and the Master, to attack Wolf. The fiery red-gold coat was symbol of a far more fiery temper. Moreover, his five years of life had changed him from the slim young playdog to a stocky little Hercules.

Small as he was and devoid of an ounce of fat, yet his muscular body weighed sixty-two pounds. Every pound was whalebone and sinew. He was a hurricane fighter;—adroit, deadly, terrible.

The Mistress sought to cry out to him to turn back, But, before the words could be spoken, Lad had flung himself once more at his presumptuous son.

The old dog's momentary vigor and prowess were gone. He could not hope to hold his own in that or any other contest;—he who once could have thrashed his weight in tigers. Yet his hero heart did not flinch. The old dog would fight on, if need be, until he was destroyed. That was Lad's nature, from birth to death. He knew no fear.

At Wolf he lurched, head lowered, his blunted and yellowed and worndown teeth lunging afresh for the gold-white throat.

Wolf sprang forward to meet and overthrow him. Then, suddenly, before the two bodies could crash together, the younger dog drew back and to one side.

In a fraction of a second he had realized who and what it was that had assailed him. He knew the pathetic weakness of the ancient collie. Lad was his sire. Lad was king of The Place's various Little People; himself among them. Lad was helpless in battle.

Whether any or all these thoughts checked his countercharge, nobody but Wolf ever knew. The fact remained that he recoiled from the half-begun assault and, head and tail up, walked quietly away. His hackles did not bristle. The lips were not curled back. No growl came from his throat. Nor, in his unruffled retreat was there a hint of fear. He simply declined battle. This for the first and last time in his life.

Lad, still shaken and indignant at the rough handling he had received, staggered after him; to punish the upset inflicted upon his dignified self.

"Lad!" called the Mistress, jumping down from the car. "*Laddie!*"

At the imperative summons, Lad halted in his advance. Reluctantly he came to the Mistress and stood looking unhappily up into her face. Also, he began at once to "talk" to her; as was his wont in moments of stress or of affection.

Nobody hearing his wordless mutters at such times could doubt Laddie was trying to speak. His grumblings and his higher notes expressed every shade of emotion, from anger to gratitude.

Now, his old voice scaled to a querulous treble as he tried to explain to his deity the humiliation that had been put upon him and her own grave fault in turning him back from his punitive expedition against Wolf.

"It's all right, Laddie dear," she explained, crooningly, as she stroked his worriedly upraised head. "He didn't mean to tease you. He was saving you from being horribly hurt; just through my carelessness. It's all right. And you're to leave him alone."

As she talked, she continued to pet Lad's head and to rumple his silken ears in the way he loved. He listened, still muttering under his breath; still glowering balefully at the retreating Wolf.

Naturally, the old dog did not understand a fifth of the Mistress's consoling words. Yet long experience had taught him to read human tones and meanings with almost incredible precision. Thus he knew now that the Mistress was forbidding him to carry this quarrel further and that she was seeking to soften his righteous anger.

His sensitive feelings were keenly hurt. Always Laddie had been supersensitive. Of late he was prone to be offended or hurt, on the slightest pretext. Finding his plaint ignored and himself forbidden to go on with the fight, he drew coldly away from the Mistress's soft touch that he loved so.

Flattening his little tulip ears back close to his head, he stalked off to his lair under the porch hammock; there to lie and grieve until someone should come to talk or pet him out of his sulks.

"Oh, dear!" exclaimed the Mistress, looking after him. "He's unhappy again. I ought to go over and make friends with him. But I ought much more go and tell Wolf what a brave thing he did. He—"

"Yes," agreed the Master. "It was the pluckiest thing I've seen any dog do;—even Laddie, in his prime. I don't mean shoving Lad out of the way of the car; but being brave enough to refuse to fight him, afterward. That took real courage, for a hot-tempered collie like Wolf. Where is he, anyhow?"

Along with Lad's pluck and Lad's wisdom, Wolf had inherited just a tinge of Lad's sensitiveness. Wolf knew, as thoroughly as did the

Mistress and the Master, that he had done well in saving Lad from the wheels and that he had shown unbelievable self-control in refusing to fight with an aged dog he could have killed with ease.

But, looking back, as ever, to the Mistress, for approval, he had seen her bending over poor old Laddie, petting and crooning to him; without a word or a glance for the real hero of the scene.

Wherefore, disgusted and cranky, Wolf pattered out of sight around the corner of the house and thence down past the stables toward the lakeside woods. As usual, he turned to the forest in his hour of unhappiness.

Out from a yard in the lower kennels beyond the barn, a half-dozen fluffy three-month-old collie pups came tearing, at sight of him. They frisked across to him, capering awkwardly about his legs, leaping up and pawing at his head and face, yelpingly exhorting him to play.

Generally, Wolf loved a romp with the successive relays of Sunnybank collie pups. Alone of all The Place's grown dogs, he relished their pawing and their clumsy onslaughts. It was pretty to see him frolic gently with them or lead them in a sweeping race or submit to their bear-like maulings.

Generation after generation of these pups he had played with, during his five years. Generation after generation, they had grown into dogs larger than he; these children and grandchildren of gigantic Bruce.

To-day, Wolf was in no mood for romping or indeed for associating with anything or anybody. He growled loudly and dramatically, to discourage the puppies' playful advances. This failing to scare them off or even to impress them, he broke into a canter. Delightedly they streamed out in a ragged pursuing line. Noting this, Wolf quickened his pace to a run; which left the fleetest of the collie babies yelping hopelessly after the gold-red meteor.

One puppy only kept up the futile race; a stubborn Teddy Bear youngster that had not sense enough to know there was no chance to catch up. On galloped the puppy; its gait like a rheumatic rocking horse's, its fluffy brain carrying but one single idea;—that of joining the red-gold collie who was its hero and who frolicked so entertainingly with it and its brethren and sisters.

Wolf reached the refuge of the woods. On he went, but now at a leisurely trot; stopping at whiles to sniff at some alluring rabbit-trail or squirrel-scent. And on, far behind, lumbered the puppy.

Past the boundaries of The Place traveled Wolf; his grievances beginning to ebb as he encountered one rabbit-track after another. The freshest of these, presently, he followed.

A furlong farther on, and at a point near the road, the track veered lakeward in a semi-circle. Wolf, following it, knew why. Scent and sound told him, minutes earlier, that people were lunching in the roadside grass. No wonder the ambling bunny had skirted the spot.

Passing within fifty feet of the lunchers, Wolf gave them a sidewise glance. They were two men and a seven-year-old boy. They had been sitting near their rattletrap little touring car: gorging food which seemed to have been wrapped in an incalculable number of greasy newspapers.

These papers now were wide-littered on the lush green grass; marring the roadside sweetness and the beauty of the summer countryside. Nor did any of the trio intend to pick them up or to clean the spot there food-fragments and eggshells and wooden dishes had defiled.

The Automobile has placed scenery-defilement (as well as immorality) within the reach of all. Thousands of folk who, of old, could not have scraped together enough ready money to hire a horse and buggy for a ten-mile drive into the country, now can and do swarm broadcast through the rural loveliness; running over dogs and chickens in the road; trespassing flagrantly; strewing the wistful landscape with the remains of their stodgy repasts.

Try to reason with them for such filthy desecration and you will learn from their truculently inspired lips that "this is a free country." Assuredly the Motorcar and not the Eagle should be the symbol of rural America's newfound "freedom."

As Wolf padded past, noiseless and unseen, behind a ragged line of underbrush, the three people were getting up from their meal and preparing to board their car. Wolf did not give them a second glance or a second thought. For here the rabbit-trail was not a minute old. Breaking into a run the dog followed it, nose to earth.

The rabbit, just ahead, heard him and dived for safety into a cranny of a tumbledown stone wall. That ended the chase; as Wolf knew by long experience. Nothing was to be gained by pawing at the wall's big stones or by barking threats to his escaped prey.

When a rabbit is so unsportsmanly as to slip into the catacomb mazes of a stone wall, there is nothing for a self-respecting collie to do but give up the hunt.

Of course Wolf could have crouched in the underbrush for several hours on the chance that the bunny might emerge again on the same side of the wall. But that was only the barest of possibilities. It did not interest Wolf in his present mood. Glumly he faced about, retracing his useless steps.

Meanwhile, as the two men were climbing into their car, the seven-year-old boy with them cried out in happy excitement:

"Daddy! Look over there! What is it, d'you s'pose?"

Ploughing a sturdy and panting way through the stiff underbrush came the puppy. Still full of the optimism of babyhood, it was continuing the search for Wolf. The going was hard and the fat little body was tired. The pup was glad enough to stop and stare interestedly at these three humans just in front.

From birth the tiny collie had known nothing but friendliness and gentle treatment from humans. Moreover, it was still at the age when a normal puppy looks on all the world as a dear friend. Wigglingly and with tail awag, it frisked up to the boy who ran forward to meet it.

"Say!" called the boy. "It's a dog, Daddy. Can I take him home and have him for mine?"

At the request the larger of the two men turned back from the car, refusal on his lips and in his heart. He was no maudlin dog lover. Nor was he minded to have his Paterson flat encumbered by stray curs.

But as his eyes rested on the pup, the refusal was choked back. This man had some knowledge of thoroughbred dogs;—not as pets but as cash assets.

Instantly, he saw that this was a high-quality collie puppy; such a puppy as might readily sell at anywhere from $100 to $150, if backed by a pedigree and an American Kennel Club registration; and which, even without those most needful assets would bring not less than $30 as a pet; or at very least $15 from some dog-and-birdstore owner who could fit out the youngster with a faked pedigree and sell it again for $50.

Approvingly the man watched his son gather the puppy into his arms; and heard him laugh happily as the collie licked his freckled face. It would be easy enough to abstract the pup from the lad's room, late at night; and tell the mourning boy that his new pet had run away.

"All right, sonny!" he assented with charming geniality. "Fetch him along. I don't know as I mind your taking him home. Only hurry up. We're late."

The boy had braced himself for a strenuous scene of pleading. Now, joyously, he clasped his new pet to his breast and came running to the car.

This was the sight which met Wolf's gaze as he repassed the tangle of underbrush on his way back from the rabbit hunt.

The boy clambered into the back seat, hugging the pudgily soft puppy so tightly in his joy, that the pressure caused the victim to yelp aloud. The plaint reached Wolf's keen ears.

Wolf was a natural watchdog, fanatically jealous of the safety of everything pertaining to The Place. Wolf also, like Lad his sire, had quick sympathy for helplessness or for distress.

Wolf spun about; and made for the departing car.

But he was at some distance from it and with rank undergrowth to plow through. Fast though he made his way through these impediments, he did not reach the road-edge until the machine was in motion and gathering speed.

The two men sat on the front seat; the boy's father driving. The boy and the puppy had the rear seat to themselves. It was the boy who first saw Wolf, charging out of the bushes, head on, for the departing automobile.

"Look, Daddy!" he shrilled. "The puppy's mamma is coming along, too."

The driver glanced back. Dashing toward them down the road, was a gold-red collie. One glance told the man this was no costly show dog to be held for reward or to sell under a falsified pedigree. Wolf was beautiful. But he had not one show-point. The profit would not be worth the risk.

The man turned back to the work of guiding his car. No sense in stopping and capturing the pursuing collie. Best get out of the neighborhood at all possible speed; lest the kidnaped puppy's owners should appear from the roadside woods and claim their property.

While an automobile intensifies fiftyfold the ease of theft, yet its license-plates have an embarrassing way of betraying a thief. The man stepped on the accelerator.

Now Wolf was fleet of foot, past the average dog—even a collie. (And no dog, save only the greyhound, can outstrip a collie in fair race.) But no mortal dog can keep up for any length of time with a fast-driven motor-car.

The flying white feet brought Wolf alongside, before the machine had reached fullest speed. He made a wild bound for the rear seat where the puppy was struggling in the grip of his young captor. But it is not easy to board a speeding car in this fashion. His forefeet clawed impotently against the top of the rear-door; then slipped. He fell heavily in the road; barely missing the nearest hind wheel; and rolled over and over.

Catlike he gathered his legs under him as he fell. In an instant he was up. Before he was fairly on his feet again, he was in motion; speeding after the receding car, heedless of bruises and pain and lost breath.

By a mad burst of speed he gained on the machine; and once again he ranged alongside. But for only a moment. The car reached its top pace. No longer was there scope for a leap at the rear door. Wolf knew that by the time he could gather himself for such a spring he must lose too much ground. Therefore, he contended himself with keeping abreast of the machine; straining his every sinew to do so.

Even this sorry achievement, presently, was denied him. Bit by bit the car drew ahead of the galloping collie. No longer was he abreast of it. Now he was behind its rear wheels; his delicate nostrils tortured by dust and monoxide gas.

Then there was more dust and less gas; as gradually the car pushed farther ahead of its toiling pursuer. Wolf's wise brain told him this chase was ridiculously hopeless. But Wolf's fearless heart and Wolf's hotly aroused temper would not let him desist from it.

Grimly he stuck to the hopeless task. These humans were stealing something that belonged to The Place. One of these humans was hurting the puppy and making it cry out. That was all Wolf needed to know.

On sped the car. It coasted down the long hill to the bridge which spans the lake. It whirred across the bridge and on toward the village. Ever behind it, though ever farther and farther behind it, galloped Wolf.

His lungs were bursting from the supreme force of his race. His muscles were working like automata, scourged on by his wrath and by his loyalty to The Place. He was in this chase to stay until he should drop dead; unless he could overhaul his quarry sooner.

Now the outskirts of the village were at hand. Once or twice the hastening car was forced to slow down somewhat to make way for automobiles coming from the opposite direction; automobiles whose occupants stared with pitying wonder at the dusty and panting collie who followed so despairingly.

"Stop and take your dog in!" bawled a kindhearted pedestrian as the car flashed past him.

The driver heard the indignant call and guessed at its meaning. Also he had noted the looks cast by drivers of such cars as he had met. He and his machine were becoming far too conspicuous.

Nobody would have given a second thought to an automobile traveling along the highroad with a boy and a puppy in its back seat. But everyone was watching the hopeless efforts of Wolf to catch up with the machine which apparently held his master. Someone was liable to jot down the number and write about the incident to the S. P. C. A. That would be an easy clue for the stolen puppy's master to follow; if the complaint should also mention the presence of the collie baby in the tonneau.

"Take the pup from Dick," he bade his brother who shared the front seat with him. "Take him and put him down out of sight between your own feet. Quick!"

His brother obeyed, lifting the puppy from the reluctant Dick's arms; and depositing the squirming baby between his own ample boots on the floor of the front seat.

Wolf noted the exchange. The negotiating of a sharp curve and the enforced slow-down while a car in front turned the same curve more carefully, had allowed the collie to shorten the distance between him and his prey. With dust-stung and bloodshot eyes he beheld the puppy lifted wrigglingly aloft and then set down on the floor in front.

The renewed glimpse of the youngster and the sound of a whimper borne to him through the whistling of the wind in his ears, lent him new speed and purpose. Wolf called on all his strained powers for a spurt.

The fates were kind to him, at last. For as the car rounded the curve its driver saw an enormous moving van, midway across the none-too-wide road and in the act of backing slowly toward a dooryard. The van was not a hundred feet ahead of the speeders.

There was no room to pass on either side; until the van should complete enough of its maddeningly slow maneuver to allow an opening. To avert a collision, Dick's father slammed on his brakes and slowed to a fuming crawl. As he did so, he looked apprehensively back over his shoulder.

The oncoming collie might be known by sight in the village. It might well cause comment if he were seen leaping and dancing frantically around a stranger's car; with evident intent of trying to climb into it.

There were more unpleasant angles to this sport of puppy-kidnaping than the man had anticipated.

Dick, meanwhile, on the rear seat, had viewed with pitying interest and growing excitement Wolf's breakneck race. The boy had voiced his own theory, at the outset. He was certain the pursuing dog was the puppy's mother who longed to be reunited with her baby son. Twice or thrice he had announced this to his unheeding father; coupled with a plea to slacken pace and let her come aboard.

Now, the car suddenly slowed almost to a standstill, and Wolf at the same time put on that final burst of speed. Dick saw his chance. Opening wide the rear door he chirped to the onrushing dog to jump in.

Wolf obeyed.

In one whirlwind bound, he whizzed through the invitingly-open doorway. But he did not stop there. His flying feet seemed scarcely to touch the floor or the seat-back as he flung himself snarlingly at the man who held the stolen puppy between his feet.

The collie's teeth raked deeply the back of the offender's neck as he lunged forward between him and the driver. Then, with a second lunge he sought the man's throat.

The driver heard his brother's hoot of horrified anguish and saw him jump up, struggling and gesticulating. He felt something furry and murderous brush past his own shoulder; and he himself gave a yell and a jump. All this in the space of a heart-beat.

Now it is not well to jump up and to lose self-possession, while one is trying to guide a car toward a narrow gap between a moving van and a roadside ditch. The jump brought the driver's toe down with much unintended vehemence on the accelerator. His upflung hands, for the instant, left the wheel.

The ill-used car proceeded to do some jumping on its own account.

Even while the driver grabbed deliriously for the wheel and while his brother with both hands sought to fend off the furiously-attacking Wolf and while Dick screeched in terror—the machine made a drunken leap at the moving van.

It struck a corner of the far-heavier vehicle, then caromed off it; the two left-hand wheels butting out beyond the ditch-edge. In another second, the car, with engine racing amid a storm of tinklingly pattering glass, was lying upside down in the ditch.

The jerk of the fall had flung Dick and Wolf clear of the wreck; they being lighter and less firmly wedged into place than either of the men. The puppy was shot out into space and landed with a soft thud against the side of the bank; with no worse harm than a wrenched shoulder. Wolf and the boy fared even better. They were tossed to the top of the low bank, side by side; coming to earth in the long grass.

The breath was jolted out of them by the impact; and they suffered a slight bruise or two. That was the extent of their injuries.

The moving van men and some people from a house were running noisily toward the upset car; as Wolf got to his feet and surveyed the wreck.

With a fence-rail, several of these humans began to upheave the smashed side of the machine. Others pulled from under it the two injured men;—one of them groaning right lamentably from a broken ankle; the other bleeding from a nasty flesh-wound in the scalp; both of them cut and bruised and jarred into hysteria.

The scene was highly interesting to Wolf. For a moment, he forgot his own shaking-up; and stood with head on one side and ears cocked, enjoying the din and action and novelty of it all. Then he heard the puppy whine. The sound recalled him to the business of the hour.

Trotting over to the pup he nosed it gently, as a signal to get up and accompany him home. There had been too much of this traffic with strange humans. The pup had been stolen. It might well be stolen again if it were not taken at once out of harm's way and piloted homeward. Wolf gave it a second and more insistent nudge.

The puppy got up; then, whimpering, sat down again; holding out its left forepaw in token of the shoulder's injury. That injury was in no way serious. Indeed, by the morrow it was cured. But it was quite enough to make its scared possessor refuse to take a single step with the wrenched member. Down sat the puppy, waving a stubby forepaw in appeal and explanation; then turning over on its back, and looking up at the puzzled Wolf with pleadingly rolling eyes.

Dick ceased from his fascinated survey of his father and uncle, at sound of the puppy's renewed whining. He half-stooped, as if to pick him up.

Now Wolf was quite ready to fight to a finish; where a grown man was concerned. But ever he had a queer gentleness with children.

He would not assail this youngster who now bent over the silly puppy. Just the same, there must be no second stealing of the little fugitive. Wolf's mind was made up. And as usual he wasted no time in getting into action.

Darting forward he caught the puppy by the slack nape of its neck. Before Dick's hand could touch the furry head, Wolf was trotting homeward, down the road; bearing tenderly between his jaws the squealing and squirming baby collie.

Nor did he cease from his self-imposed burden-bearing; on all that long return trip; save only twice when perforce he had to set down the puppy for a moment or so to ease the aching strain on his own jaws. It is no light job to lug a fat three-month puppy, protesting and kicking, all that weary distance.

Yet Wolf kept on. Wolf always kept on. That was Wolf's keynote in life. That was his unconscious motto and principle.

The Mistress was sitting on the veranda steps, arranging some flowers for the porch jardinieres, when down the drive pattered a wornout and bedraggled figure of dust and fatigue; carrying between sagging jaws a smaller figure equally bedraggled and worn out.

Depositing the puppy gently at the Mistress's feet, Wolf stretched himself out on the steps, beside her; panting and exhausted.

But his bushy tail was awag. There was a glint of mischief in his bloodshot dark eyes.

He had done a spectacular deed. And he wanted much praising.

He was dead-tired. And he wanted much petting.

He got both.

CHAPTER V: PORTIA AND A BONE

CHAPTER V: PORTIA AND A BONE

OVER in the village, a mile distant from The Place, a mischievous boy tied a can to the tail of a friendly mongrel and harried the luckless beast merrily down the road.

The dog at last, scared to panic by the clattering tin whose weight oppressed his sensitive tail-nerves and which smote against his flying legs, ran into a fence corner and cowered there, panting and foaming at the mouth.

The boy sought to dislodge him from this sorry sanctuary and start him on his way again. This he did by yanking the dog out of the corner by the tail. The mongrel, in an ecstasy of fright and pain, whizzed about and drove his teeth into the lad's arm and then snapped at his face.

The arm bite was blunted by the coat sleeve and shirt. Yet it pierced deep into the flesh, making an ugly, though not serious wound. The panic-urged teeth had raked the face so lightly as to inflict nothing worse than a few ragged scratches.

Nevertheless, the unhappy dog had sealed his own death warrant. The boy's bullcalf bellows drew others to the spot. They saw his bleeding face and his torn and red-smeared sleeve. They saw the cur, shrinking back again in his fence corner, snarling and growling; his thin body aquiver with fear.

"Mad dog!" shrilled a woman.

"MAD DOG!" echoed hysterically the fast-increasing crowd.

One unsung hero stepped back into his own house, next door; and reappeared with a shotgun. The contents of both barrels, at pointblank range, bore the poor little mongrel swiftly and mercifully beyond the reach of pain and terror and of similar effects of human civilization.

That was all. But it was enough.

It was enough to awaken in the quiet rural neighborhood the never wholly dormant dog-scare. The borough council met and decreed muzzles and other deterrents to biting. Mothers warned their children tremblingly against all stray dogs.

A lost puppy, seeking refuge from a thunderstorm in a store vestibule, was tabulated as a potential mad dog; and most courageously was shot by the store's proprietor. The new killing served to redouble the hysteria of the community.

Few are the regions where such petty occurrences have not, soon or late, started a virulent anti-dog crusade. Read any small-town paper long enough and you will come across dramatic accounts of such a campaign; backed by editorial homilies.

In due time the scare dies a natural death and folk become sane again. But, while it lasts, it claims as many victims, in proportion—and most of them as causelessly—as did France's Reign of Terror. True these victims are only dogs; not captured nobles. But they are hailed to execution on pretexts quite as flimsy.

The fire-blue lake, with its circle of soft green hills, lay between the village and The Place. Yet the dog-scare news brought keen indignation to the Mistress and the Master. Neither of them was a maudlin dog-lover. Yet both loved dogs. There is a world of difference between the two terms.

The collies, at The Place, for the most part never went to the village. Apart from Wolf and Bobby, the two car-dogs, none of them had gone thither. They were well content with the broad confines of The Place itself and with the miles of forest and of mountain that stretched away, behind it.

They were licensed, all of them. But, as they did not intrude on the populous section of the township, they wore no muzzles; nor were they kept on leash.

They had free run of The Place. The Mistress and the Master went on long forest tramps with them every day. It never occurred to these collies to go out of bounds. For, from puppyhood they had been taught the boundary-lines of their home.

Wolf was an exception. Always, Wolf had been allowed to stray where he would. Too clever to be struck down by the fastest or most erratic motor car, he was as safe on the highroad as on the veranda.

Of late years, Wolf had become more or less a law unto himself. Lad was dead. So was Bruce, the Beautiful. Wolf ruled supreme, as King of The Place's dogs. His was a venturesome and eccentric reign; not aloofly benevolent like Bruce's or Laddie's. For, in some ways, Wolf was like no other dog.

More and more utterly, with the passing of the years, he had become the loved and trusted chum of the Mistress and of the Master. He was their shadow, wherever they chanced to move; especially the Mistress's. Toward her his air of protective loyalty increased with every year.

It was his pride to ride beside her on the car-seat, when she chanced to go driving without the Master or some guest. There he would sit, erect and vigilant; be the drive ever so many hours long. If she left the car, to pay some call or to go into a store, the machine was as safe from molestation as though a troop of state police were guarding it.

Woe—swift and sudden woe—to the man who might chance to lay hand on the vehicle or to approach unduly close to it!

The more so, when the Mistress happened to be in the car. At such times, nothing but her command kept Wolf from launching himself at tradesmen or friends who might come up for a word with her. Protection of the Mistress and of the Mistress's car was a mania with the staunch little red-gold collie.

For example, a year earlier, an expressman had essayed to lift from the car's rear seat a trunk brought over to the railroad station. Before the Mistress could have time to remember the guardian-proclivities of the dog sitting beside her, the man had reached into the tonneau and had gripped the trunk—the trunk which, to Wolf's mind, was one of the sacred possessions of The Place.

In almost the same gesture, the man was jumping back, nursing a furrowed wrist, where the collie's harrowing teeth had grazed as the hand had hastily been withdrawn from the danger-zone.

The expressman—Ranson was his name—was also a dogman. To his eternal credit, Ranson did not resent the collie's attempt to safeguard the car's contents; but gave him praise for his vigilance.

The story went around the neighborhood; and folk gave the car a wider berth, thereafter, when Wolf was in it. But none thought the less of him for his zeal.

This was before the time when the village's mad-dogless mad dog scare stirred the insensate fear-swamps which lurk ever at the bottom of the human brain. For a space, during that insane era, everything was different.

It was on a morning in the very vortex of the mad dog crusade that the Mistress drove over to the village for the mail and to do the daily marketing.

The Master, being overbusy at his desk that day, did not join her as usual on the matutinal round of errands. Big Bobby, who had succeeded his sire, Bruce, as Wolf's companion in the car, also stayed at home, stretched as usual at the Master's feet, under the outdoor desk.

Monstrous proud was Wolf, as always at such times as he was the Mistress's sole escort and when he was thus allowed to sit beside her on the front seat. Pride shone in every line of his compact gold-red body.

From time to time he would turn toward the Mistress and lay one white forepaw lightly on the arm nearest him. A ride of state, alone with her, was the chiefest of Wolf's many life-joys.

The Mistress had set forth somewhat earlier than usual, from The Place. Realizing that the mail might not yet be sorted, she went first to the market. Otherwise this story would not have been written.

She had telephoned her market order in advance; and her purchases were ready. An employee of the shop came out to the car, his arms full of parcels.

These packages he placed in the tonneau. Wolf, from long experience with this, did not molest him. The man finished emptying his arms of the bundles.

Then he picked up one of the bulkiest of them. It was a bagful of bones and meat-scraps, such as were presented, thrice a week, to The Place's dogs. Out from the bag he drew a tempting bone. This he offered to Wolf; of whom he was fond.

Wolf took the bone daintily between his mighty jaws; wagging his bushy tail in recognition of the gift. Then the car started for the post office.

Now a dog does not add to the neatness nor to the cleanliness of an automobile by chewing a bone all over its front seat's cushions. The Mistress was aware of this. Yet she did not like to hurt the giver's feelings by taking the bone away from Wolf while the car was still in sight of the market.

So she drove as fast as might be to the post office, a furlong distant; before Wolf could become really engrossed in the treat.

Arriving there, she got out of the machine. Spreading a crumpled newspaper over the floor of the front part, she motioned Wolf to descend, with his treasure, to this cramped space.

"Eat it, down there, Wolfie," she ordered. "Then the car won't look quite as much as if it lived in a slaughter house."

She left him chewing happily, and went into the post office.

Apart from getting the mail there were, this morning, stamps to buy and a registered letter to sign for. So the post office visit was considerably longer than usual.

Left alone on the car-floor, Wolf ate away complacently, for a moment or so. Then, letting the bone fall between his forepaws, he glanced up, somewhat truculently.

The collie's subconscious mind, never far off guard, told him that some human had halted alongside the car. Hence his vigilantly forbidding expression as he glanced up.

The bone rolled forward, along his sloping front paws; and balanced itself precariously on the sill of the open door. Another ounce of momentum and it must have fallen to the running board and must have bounced thence to the sidewalk.

This thought occurred to the man who had stopped carelessly in his morning stroll, to see the collie gnawing the bone in the car-bottom.

The man was one Jabez Coak; an oldster who had drawn up and urged upon the borough council a recent anti-dog ordinance; and who was still noisily grouchy at the council's failure to adopt his rigid recommendations for the abatement of the local canine race.

Coak was one of those rare beings, an innate doghater. In early childhood he had sought to poke a sick and stray hound out from under the steps of his father's house. He had used a sharp-pronged rake for the purpose. The sick dog had been scraped and goaded past patience; and had flown at him, inflicting several light bites and an unforgettable nervous shock.

From that time, Coak had had a horror and hatred for all dogs. His views on the subject had brought him scant popularity in his dog-loving neighborhood; until the recent crusade had aligned him for once with the majority of his acquaintances.

He reveled in the fond belief that at last the village was to rid itself of the friendly dogs which were its pets and which were his bane.

Many a time had Jabez Coak seen Wolf, on the trips of The Place's car to the village. Indeed he had seen him, from a safe distance, when Wolf so mistakenly had snapped at Ranson, the expressman.

Wandering down the street, this morning, Coak had paused involuntarily at sight of the collie curled up in the tight space at the bottom of the machine's front seat, beside the steering wheel and emergency brake; munching the lusciously meatful bone.

To Coak it was a disgusting sight. Contemptuous fascination held him for an instant, while he watched the meal.

Then, Wolf had started up, angrily, at sight of him. And the bone had rolled forward, balancing perilously toward a fall from the doorsill to the street.

Coak saw at once the probability that this large and greasy and red-stained chunk of bone would tumble onto the immaculate walk; smearing the cleanliness of the pavement and attracting flies; besides exuding grease whereon one might readily slip and break a leg.

The man was fussily fastidious about such things. Not ten feet away stood a corrugated iron trash receptacle; one of several Coak had persuaded the borough to install for the depositing of rubbish which otherwise might have disfigured the street.

Coak looked apprehensively at the swaying bone. Wolf looked vexedly at Coak. The man did not dare take the bone from in front of the dog's forefeet and put it in the receptacle. At least, not while Wolf was eying him so forbiddingly.

Then, all at once, the collie's grim air changed in a trice to a look of happy expectancy. His uncannily keen ears had caught the vibration of the Mistress's returning step.

Turning away from the gloomily watchful Jabez Coak, the dog glanced over his shoulder toward the opening door of the post office; oblivious of everything except that his adored deity was coming back to him.

This was Coak's grand chance. He wasted no time before availing himself of it. Out darted his skinny hand; to grab the bone and to toss it into the receptacle before it should drop to the sidewalk.

He moved with much swiftness. But no creature, except perhaps a striking snake, is as quick as is the best type of collie. Wolf sensed or heard the outdarting of Coak's hand. That hand was approaching the car which it was his life-duty to protect in its owner's absence. He wheeled about, just as Jabez's fingers closed on the bone that lay on the doorsill.

Before Coak was aware that the collie had turned, Wolf's jaws had him by the wrist.

Silently, with the speed of light, the collie struck. Well it was for Coak that the cramped space crippled the dog's lunge. As it was, the jaws clamped shut, not on the bare skin of the wrist; but upon the tough cloth of the sleeve-edge.

Even so, the wrist was pinched as in a vise. The keen teeth, too, shore their way through the thick cloth and into the flesh, before the howling man could wrench free his bitten arm and reel backward.

"Wolf!" cried the Mistress, who had come out on the post office steps just in time to witness the ultra-brief attack and its cause.

At her imperative call, Wolf checked himself almost in mid-air as he was preparing to launch his muscular body from the car to the man's throat. He stood, where he was, looking like a red-gold statue of arrested motion. The Mistress hurried forward.

"Your mad dog has bit me!" yelled Coak, beside himself with hurt and fright; as he nursed the injured wrist and stared glassy-eyed on the two or three shallow teethmarks. "He's mangled my arm; and he's broke it."

To prove this he flourished the wounded wrist in her face. At the motion, Wolf fancied he saw threat to his worshiped Mistress. Once more he prepared to launch himself upon the man. And again the Mistress's warning word held him where he was.

"Back, Wolf!" she ordered; then, to Coak: "I'm terribly sorry he hurt you. But no bones in your arm or wrist are broken. If they were, you couldn't possibly move it like that. Go to the drugstore, across there; and have the teeth-marks washed out with hot water. Then dry them and paint them thickly with iodine. In less than a week they'll be well. Don't be frightened. There isn't any danger."

The man fairly gobbled at her in his terrified fury.

"No danger?" he screeched. "No *danger?* Hydrophoby isn't any danger, hey? No dan—?"

"Hydrophobia!" repeated the Mistress in mockery. "I don't know much about hydrophobia. Nobody seems to. But I do know you can't get it from a perfectly healthy dog like Wolf. And even if he had rabies, his teeth went through your sleeve, first. That would absorb any poison. You're in no danger, Mr. Coak. I'm sorrier than I can say, that Wolf should have—"

"And you'll be sorrier yet!" Coak fairly spat at her. "You'll be sorrier yet, when that rabid cur of yours is killed. He's been a menace to this c'munity, too long. If there's a law in the land, here's where he dies. He—"

The Mistress looked about her, to find that a compact crowd had sprung up from nowhere and was surrounding the car, curiously eying the scene's three actors.

To avert further howled threats from Coak and to get away from such unwelcome publicity, she set the car in motion and drove off; leaving the ever-more furious Jabez bellowing threats and death-promises after her.

Home she went. There she told the Master the sordid story.

"It wasn't Wolf's fault, one bit," she concluded. "He was lying there, gnawing the bone and not bothering anybody. Then Coak stopped to watch him. Wolfie glanced up. But he didn't go for him. I saw it through the glass door of the post office. Then Wolf heard me and looked around. And Coak stole his bone away from him. Wolf grabbed him by the wrist, for doing it. I don't blame him, one bit. He—"

Her husband's longdrawn low whistle of annoyance interrupted the narrative.

"I'll drive over there," said the Master. "I'll find Coak, and try to pacify him. Perhaps he'll have cooled down by the time I get there. If I offer him twenty dollars and say it's to pay doctors' bills for his scratched wrist, there's always a chance he may let the matter drop. I don't count on it, mind you," he added. "In fact I should say the odds are something like fifty-toone against. But it seems to be the only thing I can do about it. If he chooses to make trouble, we're all in a pretty bad fix."

"How do you mean?" asked the Mistress, worriedly. "Why, what can he do? The bite is only skin deep. It's the pinching that hurt him worst. He can't collect very heavy damages for that, can he?"

"He can collect more than damages," was the Master's morbidly glum reply. "He may be able to collect Wolf. That's what's bothering me. Not the chance of having to pay out a few dollars. I'm thinking of Wolf."

"Wolf!" echoed the Mistress.

"Yes. Don't you see? You know how the village is buzzing with the dog-scare epidemic. Well, people are as abnormal when they're scared as they are when they're drunk. It's community-psychology; just as national psychology sways people. Remember, in the war, how abnormal everyone was? Dozens of men were slugged or insulted on the streets, by strangers; because they were speaking German. Vanderslice tells me the names of thousands of honest American patriots were sent to the Military Intelligence Department by their fellow-citizens with charges that they were spies.

"All the lights were ordered put out, in New York City, one night in 1918, for fear of a German air-raid—when there wasn't a German bombing plane within three thousand miles. In the Civil War, too, a negro orphan asylum was burned and innocent negroes were hanged from lamp-posts in New York, during the Draft Riot of '63.

"Yet normal people don't burn asylums; or charge their innocent friends with being spies; or do any of those other crazy things. They do it, because their community or country is crazed by some big emotion. Well, in a lesser way, it's just the same, now, over in the village. The dog-scare makes them as merciless as all scared people are. Wolf—"

"But what can be done to him?" asked the troubled Mistress.

"Ordinarily," said the Master, "even if Coak tried to be nasty about it, there'd be no worse danger than a petty civil suit. But just now, all dogs here exist on suffrance. They're lucky when they can exist at all. The slightest hint of danger from one of them—and a death sentence is passed. If the village can be made to think Wolf is a menace, he'll be ordered shot."

"Shot!" exclaimed the Mistress, aghast. "Do you mean—?"

"I mean, unless I can persuade Coak to let it drop, the chances are all that a judicial order will be issued for Wolf's death."

"They shan't kill him," said the Mistress; speaking very quietly indeed, but with a queer tone of finality.

"No," agreed the Master. "They shan't. You're right, about that. Not if I have to declare The Place in a state of siege; or smuggle him over into New York, for a while. You can rest easy on that. The dog would give his life for either of us. And I'm not going to let him be harmed; —law or no law. Wolf means more to me than any other animal living and more than most humans do. Just the same, we're in for a nice spell of trouble-weather on his account."

Wolf, hearing his name reiterated so often, had risen from his corner of the veranda and had come across to where the Mistress and the Master stood beside the car.

To him the occurrence with Coak was a small thing and already half forgotten. But his oddly psychic nature noted the worry in the voices and faces of his deities; and, collie-like, he yearned to help them.

Wherefore, standing between the two, he looked wistfully from face to face, his soul shining unhappily in his dark eyes. He whined softly, far down in his furry throat. The Mistress laid a caressing hand on his head.

"Poor old Wolfie!" she said. "You've always been a storm-center, haven't you? But you're the dearest dog alive. And you're going to keep on staying alive. Master says so. He—"

"I'll run over and try to reason with Friend Coak," put in the Master, climbing into the waiting car. "I read once about somebody who tried to 'amuse the unamusable.' It wasn't a patch on my present job of 'reasoning with the unreasonable.' Still, it can't do any harm to make the attempt. No, Wolf!" as the dog delightedly made as though to jump into the front seat at his side. "This is one time when a collie's place is in the home. I think the village has seen enough of you for one day. Coak won't be more inclined to listen to reason, with you there to remind him of his bite."

Back to The Place returned the Master a half hour later. Crestfallen, sulky, he made report to his wife.

"The man's simply raging," he said. "It would be easier to argue with a charging bull. He swears he'll have the dog killed by law and that he'll bring civil suit against us for $20,000 for the injuries he has received. Dr. Colfax had just dressed his wrist. I asked Colfax how badly it was hurt. He says the pinch didn't cause even a sprain and that the teeth-incisions weren't a quarter-inch deep. He told Coak there is no danger; just as *you* told him. But Jabez is parading around the streets with his arm in a sling; and breathing forth threatenings and slaughter.

"And he's been to both magistrates and he's phoned to Paterson for a lawyer. I talked to him. He didn't talk back. He shrieked back. The old fellow is genuinely scared and furious. But behind all that I'm pretty sure he has an eye to the main chance, about that $20,000. Well, there's nothing we can do but wait. Unless you think it would be wiser for us to take Wolf up to the boarding kennels in Suffern. That's across the state line. He'll be safe there."

"He'll be miserably unhappy there," corrected the Mistress. "Besides, Wolf has never yet run away from anything. Why should we show less pluck than he does? Let's all three stay and fight it out."

Such amazing advice from the gentle Mistress made her husband stare at her in wonder. Then, infected by her courage, he made answer:

"You're right. We'll fight it out. But we're in for a losing fight."

The first gun of the battle was fired, a little after noon. The Master's old friend and fishing crony, Maclay, borough justice of the peace, called up on the telephone, just before lunchtime.

"This is unofficial," said he, embarrassedly. "But I've been doing unofficial things, all morning. For one thing, I refused to sign a warrant for an officer to go over to your house and shoot Wolf. Coak demanded it; and he threatens to get me impeached for refusing. It was easier to refuse; because every member of the police force here is too much of a white man to relish the job of killing such a dog as Wolf."

"Thanks," said the Master, his heart heavy. "It was good of you, Mac. Your police, over there, *are* white men; from the chief down. What—?"

"Then," pursued Maclay, "I refused to have a summons served on you and your wife. I said there was no need; and that you'd both come here to court at my request."

"We will," answered the Master.

"Coak has been at me to do about a dozen other things in regard to the case," continued Maclay. "Some of them were idiotic, but one or two of them were within his rights. I've kept on refusing. But now he's got a lawyer up from Paterson—a chap whose reputation isn't any too savory, but who knows his business and who is keen for the big contingent fee that Coak offers. He demands a hearing at two o'clock this afternoon. Will it be convenient for you people to come over to court at that time? Can you get in touch with your lawyer by then? If you can't. I'll put the case back till to-morrow morning. But I've refused so many things they wanted done—"

"Wait a second, Mac," said the Master.

Turning from the telephone, he told the Mistress the gist of Maclay's talk. She had come into the study at the sound of Maclay's name. Under her arm was a big calfskin book; part of her father's law-library. Among these books she had been browsing for the past three hours.

The Master had noticed her, curled up in a window seat, amid a score of the dusty books. But as she had an inherited love for solving legal tangles and often amused herself by such odd excursions into lawbooks, he had paid scant heed to her occupation.

"Please say that we'll be there," she said, when the Master finished telling her the request.

"We'll be there, Mac," reported the Master hanging up the receiver.

"I told him so," he went on, to his wife. "But I think it would have been wiser to wait. Even if we can get hold of Houman or a good Paterson lawyer, by two o'clock—remember this lawyer of Coak's has had all morning to prepare his case. He—"

"We won't get any lawyer," she decreed, calmly.

"Hold on!" exclaimed the Master. "Maclay is a good friend of ours, and all that. But, when he's on the bench, friendship flies out of the window. He'll judge our case, just as he'd judge an outsider's. You know that. He runs his court in a mighty informal way. You saw that, when Laddie was up before him, years ago, on that sheep-killing charge. But he dispenses 100 per cent justice. No higher court has ever reversed a decision of his; and no higher court ever will. Our being friends of his won't help us. Better let me phone to Houman or to—"

"If you don't mind," she urged, gently, "I'd rather handle the case myself."

"You?"

"Why not? Wolfie is my dog. And the law allows a layman to conduct his own defense, doesn't it; if the layman wants to. I think I'd rather do it than have a lawyer. The lawyer would know a million times more than I know. But he would *care* a million times less. That makes all the difference in the world."

Twenty-odd years of married life had taught the Master that his wife had a queer way of being in the right; even when her ideas seemed to his masculine mind the most illogical. Thus, though with no hope at all for her success, he yielded the point.

The little courtroom was full to suffocation, that afternoon, when the Mistress and the Master entered it. A policeman made a path to them to the less crowded space inside the rail, where sat Jabez Coak and his lawyer and Maclay and the court clerk.

A hum of excited interest greeted the arrival of Wolf's owners. As they came inside the rail Jabez favored them with a glower which would have done credit to Richard III and Herod, combined. Coak's arm was in a sling and was adorned by mountainous white bandages which already were beginning to lose their pristine cleanness.

The plaintiff's lawyer arose and made a most dramatic speech to the judge. In the course of it he touched on the peril of allowing ferocious dogs to live. He cited instances wherein helpless children had been hideously mangled by such brutes.

He went on to depict the awful mystery of rabies and its fatal effects on mankind. He scored the silly sentimentality which leads humans to harbor potential sources of rabies.

Then, waxing less general in his remarks, he related in gory detail the case of Jabez Coak; an honored resident of that fair community, who, during a peaceful morning walk, had been set upon and dangerously bitten by a possibly rabid collie; thus receiving "abrasions, contusions, and mental and physical anguish."

He wound up his speech by a fervid demand for a court order "for the instant destruction of this incurably vicious collie; which is a perpetual menace to the health and welfare and life of the community."

When he sat down, another murmur ran through the crowded room. His throng of hearers had never dreamed that their loved dogs were such dangers and pests. As a whole, the crowd received the speech in something like angry derision. A few were visibly impressed.

Then the Mistress arose.

"In the first place, Your Honor," she said, her low voice carrying throughout the small room, though she stood facing Maclay, with her back to the audience, "In the first place, as Your Honor knows, the law permits every dog one bite. In other words, the law holds that a first attack on a human being does not indicate that a dog is vicious. Here," handing Maclay one of the several slips of paper she held, "here is a partial list of the authorities I have looked up, to prove that. The complaint says Wolf is an 'incurably vicious dog.' But the law—"

"If it please Your Honor," spoke up Coak's lawyer, "that ruling does not obtain here. (I am not alone in my belief that it is an outworn remnant of the ancient Common Law, which should long ago have been repealed.) It does not obtain here. We anticipated some such claim; and we are prepared to prove by several reputable witnesses that this dog, Wolf—who merits his savage name of 'Wolf' if ever a dog did—attacked and bit at least one other person in this borough. To wit, John X. Ranson, an expressman. This we can establish, past doubt, *if*—"

"There is no need," returned the Mistress. "I concede it. Only, Ranson was fair enough to admit that Wolf did only what he thought was his duty in guarding our car. I was not certain that instance would be brought up. So I mentioned the law that protects harmless dogs from fanatics by giving them a second chance."

She glanced again at the sheaf of notes in her hand, then said:

"If Your Honor will hunt up the precedents I've indexed on this second bit of paper, you will see that the law holds an automobile to be private and personal property, as much as a house is regarded as private and personal property. It holds than an automobile may be considered as its owner's home, insofar as 'right of search' and other 'domiciliary rights' are concerned."

She handed Maclay the slip of paper, covered with jottings.

"That is established," said the judge, waving back the proffered slip. "But the court fails to see what bearing—"

"Just a minute, please," begged the Mistress, consulting her notes afresh. "There is another point the law has decreed. Here are some of the decisions—all I could find in such a short time. The latest of them, you will notice, is a decree handed down by Judge Sylvain J. Lazarus of California, in the case of—"

"Your Honor," fumed the lawyer, "I object to—"

"Objection overruled," said Maclay. "Your opponent has full right to cite any precedent which has a bearing on this case. Until the court is convinced that such precedent has no direct bearing on it, no objection will be sustained."

He nodded to the Mistress to proceed. Handing him the third slip of paper, she went on:

"A collie, in San Francisco, bit a boy who took away from him a bone the dog was gnawing. The case came before Judge Lazarus. The judge, as reported in the local papers, handed down this decision that a friend of my husband's sent to us as a curiosity, a year or two ago:"

From one of several newspaper clippings she read aloud:

"Judge Lazarus rendered the following interesting verdict:—'This dog has done nothing to deserve death. The evidence has established that he was gnawing on a bone. That bone was the dog's own property. Any stranger trying to deprive a dog of such property has violated the latter's property rights; and such act constitutes an invasion which the dog has a right to prevent with force. No one—' "

"Your Honor!" cried the lawyer, "I object to this as irrelevant, immaterial and incompetent. There is no—"

"Overruled," said Maclay. "Proceed, Madam."

" 'No one,' " the Mistress continued her reading of the decree, " 'no one would condemn a man who should forcibly prevent a burglar from stealing his property. The dog's provocation was as great, in its way, as would be that of a man repelling a thief. Had I and any other man been in the dog's place, undoubtedly we should have sought at all hazards to protect our endangered property. This case is dismissed.'

"This case of ours," pursued the Mistress's soft voice, as she laid aside the clipping, "is wholly similar to the one tried before Judge Lazarus; so far as the Lazarus case goes. The other precedents which I have indexed from lawbooks and which Your Honor can verify—all bear out the same verdict.

"Now then, there is another angle to this. We can prove by any number of onlookers that Wolf was in our car, this morning, and that the bone was also in our car. I think the prosecution won't deny that."

"We concede that," said the lawyer, impatiently; adding in forensic appeal: "Your Honor, I protest that the time of the court is being tampered with and wasted by this unusual, pointless—"

"The court is the best judge of how the court's time is used," rebuked Maclay; and he nodded again to the Mistress to proceed.

"Your Honor has been good enough to agree that a man's automobile is, for the time, his home," resumed the quiet voice. "Very good. The case seems to me to stand like this:—Wolf was in his owner's 'home,' this morning. He was eating a bone, there—a bone which we can prove had been given freely to him; and which therefore was his property. He—"

The lawyer hopped excitedly to his feet. He caught at last the drift of the defense; and he was eager to stem its course. Maclay motioned him back. The Mistress continued:

"Wolf was in his master's 'home,'—on guard in that 'home.' He was eating a bone which was his own property. Mr. Coak came along and trespassed—at least his right hand and arm trespassed—on the 'home' which Wolf had been taught to guard.

"More;—Mr. Coak forcibly stole—or attempted to steal—from that home something which belonged in it and which, incidentally, belonged to Wolf. In his capacity of watchdog, as well as in his capacity as owner of the bone, Wolf defended our home and his own property; in the only way a dog can.

"The law holds further (here are the authorities on that point) that a dog is his master's absolute property and that anything belonging to the dog also belongs to his owner. For instance, if you give a jeweled collar to my dog, there are two legal precedents which say that that collar thus becomes mine.

"Very good. The car was my temporary home. The bone, being given to my collie, belonged by law to me. Mr. Coak invaded my home in my absence; and, by his own admission, attempted to steal therefrom an article of personal property which belonged to me. My dog attempted to protect my home and my property. This he did, without leaving that home. If he is to be shot for guarding his owner's home and property, then every dog, henceforth, that defends his master's house from a midnight burglar, must legally be shot."

"Nonsense!" ejaculated the lawyer, jumping up again. "Your Honor, I protest against—"

"Go on, Madam," decreed Maclay; adding to the lawyer: "You are at liberty of course to except to my rulings. You know that. The clerk will note any exceptions."

"Also," said the Mistress, "if Wolf is to be killed for what he did, the very same evidence that condemns him will serve as irrefutable evidence in the criminal charge of forcible entrance and attempted theft, which we will then make against Mr. Coak.

"It was a shock to me to see Mr. Coak intrude so lawlessly on my temporary home, this morning," she finished, keeping her face straight and her voice steady, by marked effort. "It was a shock to me to see him commit such flagrant trespass. It was a far more severe shock to me to see him commit attempted robbery in that home. I have not yet recovered from that shock. So, apart from the criminal charges which we can make, I am quite certain I have grounds for civil suit, in heavy damages, against him. He caused me much 'mental and physical anguish.' . . . That is all, Your Honor."

She sat down, demurely, beside the Master. There was a rustle and a multiple excited whispering among the spectators. Jabez Coak was leaning forward, whispering sputteringly in the ear of the disgruntled lawyer. Maclay cleared his throat to speak.

Before the first word could come, the rustle in the room increased with loud suddenness. People were hitching their chairs to one side or another and craning their necks and exclaiming.

Up the short aisle, thus created, ambled a red-gold collie; tail awag, eyes dancing with mischief.

Wolf, left at home in the study, had wearied of loneliness. A maid opened the study door to answer the telephone. Wolf slipped out, past her; and began to search for his owners.

Instantly, he caught the scent of the car's old tires—a scent such as is familiar to more dogs than may seem probable. He had heard the machine depart, a half hour earlier. He had received no command to stay at home. He had been merely left in the study,—by chance, for all he could know. Off he went on the fresh trail.

At the courthouse's open door he found the car; and he caught the far fresher track of his deities' footsteps. He cantered gleefully up the untended stairs and into the courtroom.

There, at sight of the Mistress and the Master, he frisked up the aisle and in a light bound cleared the law railing. In another instant, he was standing beside the Mistress; looking for all the world like a delightedly mischievous child whose mischief has brought him to a desired goal.

At a motion from the Mistress, he dropped down at her feet; his bushy tail still brushing the floor in joyous wags; his eyes wandering in friendly interest around the strange room.

"Your Honor," said the Mistress, gravely, "My client is in court. May I apologize for his unceremonious entrance? This is the 'incurably vicious' dog Mr. Coak wants killed. Your Honor will note he has just trotted through a crowd of people, with his tail wagging and with no attempt to harm any of them."

At the faintly mocking note in her voice, Wolf's tail began to wag with fresh zest. Somebody laughed. The laugh was taken up. Then the mirth changed into a multiple gasp of dread.

One of the women spectators in the front row of chairs had brought along with her a three-year-old baby, too young and too adventurous to be left safely at home alone.

The baby, tiring of the dull proceedings, had wriggled down from her mother's lap and had crawled unnoticed through the wide-parted railings, to the space in front of the bench.

Scarce had the child arrived in this forbidden ground than a highly fascinating red-gold dog had also entered the space within the rail and had lain down within a few feet of her.

With a squeal of joy, the baby toddled over to Wolf, and threw both chubby arms around his neck. The squeal drew all eyes to the spot.

The sight of the helpless youngster embracing the murderous dog, sent a gasp of horror through the room. Men sprang to their feet. Women cried aloud. Then followed a confused forward surge; and almost directly a still more confused halt, as the tension slumped.

For Wolf had greeted the baby with rapture. He loved little children and was never so happy as when one of them found a chance to play with him.

The horrified spectators beheld the child climb athwart Wolf's muscular back; and, seizing his furry ears for reins, dig her heels into his sides and cry:

"Giddap, horsey!"

Wolf, grinning idiotically, wagged his tail until it threatened to fall off. Twisting back his head, he tried to lick the exultant baby face just above him.

The rabidest dog-hater could not have looked on and have believed the crowing baby was in any more peril than would she have been in her own crib.

"Your Honor," said the Mistress, meekly, "our 'incurably vicious' dog seems to have used up his whole day's supply of incurable viciousness, on Mr. Coak. He—"

A roar of laughter from the audience drowned her words—the laughter of stress-relief as much as of merriment.

Maclay hammered fiercely with his gavel for order. In the moment's hush which followed he rasped out his verdict:

"*Case dismissed!*"

CHAPTER VI:
THE MYSTERY-SHOW

CHAPTER VI: THE MYSTERY-SHOW

DARIUS MADDEN had never heard of Wolf. Byron Deene had never heard of Wolf nor of Darius Madden. Madden had never heard of Byron Deene. Wolf had heard of neither of them; nor would he have bothered his head to remember them. They were not of the type that dogs care for. And the fiery little red-gold collie cared for nobody on earth except only the Mistress and the Master.

Yet Fate linked the two human strangers and the dog together, for one eventful day—linked them in Fate's own whimsical fashion.

A mere handful of years had wrought wide changes in the canine population of The Place. Grand old Lad lived out his span of sixteen years and was buried in a shady corner of the grounds (whither, in later days, more than two thousand humans in all—for reasons best known to themselves—chose to make pilgrimages).

Bruce, the Beautiful, had shared the rear seat of the car with Wolf, for two years after Laddie's death; and had taken the old collie's position as King of The Place's dogs. Then Bruce, too, had died; and thereby the Master lost a pal whose flawless beauty and brain and loyalty left an un-fillable gap.

So it was that Wolf, at eight years old, became acknowledged king of The Place's dogs, ruling his subjects with a dash and a gay swiftness of discipline that left no doubt as to his rank among them nor of his realization of it.

His savage temper of earlier days was softening. Others, now, besides the Mistress and the Master, could venture to pet him without risking a slashed wrist. True, he paid no heed to outsiders. Yet no longer did he resent their civil advances. Among The Place's many dogs he chose almost no friends, save Bruce's big son, Bobby, his new seat-mate in the car.

More and more, in the past few years, had Wolf become the close chum of the Mistress and the Master. Now that Lad and Bruce were gone, he was first in the hearts of these human deities of his. And the knowledge made him monstrous proud and happy. Never, for ten minutes, during the entire day, was he absent from one or both of his deities.

During these later years, he developed queer psychic traits, which a score of persons can vouch for, but which none can explain. For example, one morning, during a sojourn in town, the Mistress and the Master decided, at breakfast, to run up to The Place for the day. The Master arose from the table to telephone The Place's superintendent to have a car meet the next train. Before he could reach the instrument, the phone bell rang. At the other end of the wire, the superintendent asked:

"You're coming up here to-day, aren't you, sir?"

"How did you know?" asked the bewildered Master.

"Wolf told me," was the amazing response. "A couple of minutes ago he began to dance around as if he was crazy. Now he's galloped down to the Big House and he's scratching to go in. He always does that when you're coming home. I don't know how he finds it out."

Yes, the incident sounds fishy—except to those who know the psychic mind of the highest type of collie. Yet it is true. And other and stranger true anecdotes of the sort might be told of the strange little red-gold dog. For example, his voicing of an eerie death-yell, repeated over and over again, at the precise time when someone dear to The Place died, fifty miles away.

All of which is a digression from the tale of Wolf's brief linking-up with Darius Madden and Byron Deene; but which perhaps is interesting in its own way and assuredly is true.

The success of the annual Tuxedo dog-shows led the folk of Greenwold Manor to tempt publicity and fame by a similar exhibition.

The time was September. The scene was the race-track, behind the Greenwold Manor clubhouse. It was to be an open-air show and for charity. A press-agent was hired. The Manor's cottagers were levied upon for expense money and for cash "specials." An American Kennel Club license was secured for the show. The Manorites went to work with a zeal which, aimed in any other direction, would have netted their charity a banner sum.

Darius Madden was President of the Manor's club, having been elected a month earlier to that glittering office in face of a whirl-wind opposition. The dog-show was his own idea. It was one of several spectacular measures whereby he planned to impress the wisdom of his election as President on the whole community.

Darius Madden was a Live Wire. He admitted it. Also Darius Madden had more money than he needed and almost as much money as he wanted. He spent cash most lavishly in promoting the show.

His wife, just then, was mourning the demise of an asthmatic old collie she had bought long before at a bird-store—a collie sold to her as a fluffy puppy, and provided with a pedigree which the birdstore man had copied laboriously from a battered studbook which he kept for just such emergencies. He gave the nameless pup a sire whose name was once a watchword in dogdom. (True, this alleged sire had died some seven years before the pup was born, but Mrs. Madden was so proud of his name on the pedigree that she had the fairytale document framed.)

Urged thereto by his grieving wife, Madden now offered several costly "specials," to be awarded to collies at the forthcoming show. One of these was a twenty-dollar silver vase, to go to "the oldest and best-cared-for collie." Mrs. Madden had seen such a prize offered at the Madison Square Garden Show, in New York; and the memory of it had remained with her. Now, at her behest, her husband made a similar offer.

Furthermore, he put up a two-hundred-dollar sterling silver bowl, to be awarded to the show's best collie of either sex. He scattered a handful of cash specials, ranging from $5 to $15 through the premium list, to be won by other collies. But the prizes which stood forth most garishly were the two-hundred-dollar bowl for the best collie and the twenty-dollar cup for oldest-and-best-cared-for.

Not at haphazard had Darius Madden offered these two pieces of silverware. The twenty-dollar cup had been suggested by his wife, in memory of her own defunct dog. It was a whim of hers. But Mrs. Madden was a woman of iron whim; and her husband long ago had learned to obey her rather than to serve as "feeder" in a dramatic dialogue.

But there had been real method in Madden's offer of the $200 bowl. His strongest, if most fickle supporter, in the election for presidency, had been his rotund neighbor, Colonel Rothe. On the temperamental colonel he relied for reelection and for many intermediate favors.

Rothe had just bought, at a criminal price, that renowned international champion collie, Hector of Pogis; an imported dog that had swept the show circuit a few months earlier and was considered by experts to be the best collie in the United States.

There could be scant doubt as to Hector's victory at the Manor show; especially as he chanced to be in luxuriant coat at this autumn season when most of his breed are all-but hairless. Thus, by his glittering offer, Madden hoped to grapple the colonel's approval to himself, if not "with hooks of steel" at least with a bowl of sterling silver. It was a pretty plan—and almost sportsmanly withal, compared with some of the stunts perpetrated in connection with dogshow-prizes.

Which brings us, by prosy degrees, to Byron Deene.

On the strength of a fairly accurate knowledge of Chihuahua toy dogs, Deene had received a judging license. It was granted on the supposition that he would use it for no other purpose than for the occasional judging of Chihuahuas.

Deene was the official brother-in-law of the Chairman of the Greenwold Manor dogshow's bench committee. At a meeting of that committee, he was chosen as Chihuahua judge for the forthcoming show. Then, as three consecutive collie judges declined the invitation to adjudicate their special breed at that time, the committee complimented its chairman by asking Deene to add collies to Chihuahuas.

Deene had a refreshing ignorance concerning collies; and indeed of nineteen dog-breeds out of twenty. But he had an equally refreshing faith in himself to give wise decisions on any and all canine matters. So, obligingly, he consented to judge collies at Greenwold, in addition to his beloved and ultra-tiny Chihuahua proteges. A similar thing has been done too often to call for comment.

Premium lists of all shows are sent broadcast to people known to be interested in exhibiting dogs. Thus, a fortnight before the Greenwold Manor event, such a pamphlet found its way to The Place.

The Master riffled its pages carelessly in search of the section devoted to collies. Down the luring list of specials strayed his eye. He felt no personal interest in the proffered awards. None of The Place's high-quality collies was in good enough coat, just then, to stand any chance of victory at a well-contested show. And to show an out-of-coat collie is to court defeat.

In another three months a half-dozen of them would be carrying luxuriantly massive winter coats. At present, they were none of them in show-form. None but Wolf.

Wolf's short harsh red-gold coat was in its full prime. But that was all the good it was likely to do him. For, Wolf most decidedly was not a show dog. Handsome and wise and fearless he was. But none of those things count in a dog-show.

The standard calls for a classically wedge-shaped head: Wolf's head was short and broad. The standard calls for smallish and slightly slanted eyes: Wolf's eyes were big and round. (It did not matter that his eyes were alight with sense and with fun and with staunchness and that a soul shone behind them. They were not the eyes of a show collie.) The standard calls for a long coat of certain texture: Wolf's coat was like a chow's. His tail was a timber-wolf's, not a collie's. His figure was powerfully stocky; not greyhound-like in symmetrical line and curve.

No, Wolf had not one show-point, despite all his brain and looks. So it profited nothing that his coat was in full bloom, alone of all The Place's collies.

As the Master neared the end of the list of special prizes in the collie section, he read aloud:

" *'Special 198: Silver Cup (Value $20) For Oldest and Best-Cared-For Collie.'* "

The Mistress looked up with sudden interest. "There's Wolfie," she said.

"Where?" asked the Master, stupidly.

"I mean," she explained, "he's nearly nine years old. And he is in wonderful condition, His teeth are as white and strong and perfect as they were seven years ago. You said yourself that a dog is as old as his teeth. Wolf has the teeth of a puppy. And he doesn't show a sign of age anywhere. I don't believe there's another eight-year-old collie in New Jersey that is so young, all over. There won't be a single collie at Greenwold that carries his years as well."

The Master blinked at her, scarce understanding her drift.

"Don't you see?" she went on. "Wolf would be almost certain to win that cup. Any collie judge could see he is in the best condition, for his age, and—"

"Any collie judge could see," interrupted the Master, "that Wolf combines in his own head and body and tail every possible defect a show dog could have. And," he added, defiantly, half to himself, "I wouldn't swap him for every show-champion on earth."

"Neither would I," declared the Mistress, overhearing the muttered speech. "Neither would anyone who had the wit to understand his brain and his loyalty and his queer lovableness. Why can't somebody invent shows where dogs are judged by their cleverness and dispositions and staunchness and by all the million things that make them worth more than any mere money? Why must they always be judged as if they were prize cattle or pigs;—just by a few show-points that have nothing to do with a dog's worthwhileness? Wolf is—"

She stopped, her ear arrested by a rhythmic beat that broke in on her words. Wolf was curled up, on the veranda; just behind her chair and in constant danger of a raking from its rockers. At the repeated sound of his name he came out of his light doze and called attention to his own presence by pounding his bushy tail on the porch floor.

He followed this demonstration by getting lazily to his feet, stretching fore and aft, and then coming forward. He stood midway between the Mistress and the Master; and thrust his cold blunt nose into the Mistress's hand.

"Do you want to go to a nice dog-show, Wolfie?" she asked him. "Do you want to go there and win a nice bright silver—or almost silver —cup for being old and well-cared for? Do you?"

The collie's eyes danced, at the note of query in her loved voice. The collie's sturdy snow-white feet began dancing, too. Wolf did not understand the trend of the questions, of course; though he had an uncanny comprehension of human speech. Indeed, by actual fair test, his owners once proved that he had an accurate knowledge of no fewer than forty-three simple words and phrases.

But he knew the Mistress was asking if he wanted to do something-or-other. That galvanized him into sudden interest. The fact that he did not grasp the full import of her query brought to his eyes a queerly wistful look as of someone who seeks to catch a phrase whose meaning barely escapes him. There was pathos in the look; the pathos of brute or of human who strives vainly to break through a mental barrier.

"I verily believe he'd love to go," said the Master, watching the dog. "As a rule, our collies hate shows. But Wolf is so crazy about showing off, and he turns everything new into such thrilling drama—I believe he'd be as wild over it as a kid at a circus. We'll take him, if you want to, so much. The only trouble is—"

"There's always 'trouble' about everything jolly," spoke up the Mistress, as her husband paused. "How nice that there's only one 'trouble' about this! What *is* the 'only trouble'?"

"Why," said the Master, "to enter him for any of the special prizes at a show, the rule says we'll have to enter him in some 'regular' class, too. Had you thought of that? Of course, we can just enter him as a Novice. That's by far the easiest class. But even there, every collie with any pretensions to show-type will beat him. I'm silly enough to hate to take the little old dog into the ring, to be beaten by a bunch that haven't half his looks or a tenth of his sense. Still—"

"Still," summed up the Mistress, "he's sure to win the twenty-dollar cup, later on. And *we'll* know he's the grandest dog there, even if the judge doesn't. By the way, who is to be the collie judge at Greenwold?"

The master rifled the premium list again.

"There's no specialty judge for them," he reported, presently. "They —Oh, here it is! *'Mr. Bryon Deene: Chilhuahuas and Collies.'* It—"

"Chihuahuas *and* collies?" echoed the Mistress. "What a combination! It's like one man judging hummingbirds and eagles. I —"

"I never heard of this man, Deene," mused the Master. "I thought I knew at least the name of every collie judge and of every all-round judge who handles collies. Byron Deene is a novelty to me. . . . Anyhow, we'll take Wolf there, if you and he say so. How about it, Wolf?"

At Greenwold, the Mistress and the Master found a goodly quota of collie-breeders. In spite of the poor time of year for showing long-haired dogs, yet the many cash specials, as well as the cash prizes in regular classes, had brought forth no fewer than nineteen collies;—a "three-point show" for the lucky winner. Among all the owners, none knew Byron Deene. One or two had a vague memory of reading his name in former show-catalogs. But they knew nothing of him. Chihuahua breeders and collie breeders have scant common ground whereon to meet.

From the first instant, the show was a delight to Wolf. The presence of several hundred dogs of all breeds, and the din of their multiple barks and yelps, did not frighten him. They spelt excitement, as did the hurrying throngs and the unwonted surroundings. Excitement was Wolf's chief life-joy.

Unafraid, eager, vibrant, his eyes gay and his tail awag, he danced alongside the Mistress to his numbered bench; and from that vantage point he proceeded to investigate with lively interest the collies to either side of him and the passing spectators.

"Look at Wolfie!" exclaimed the Mistress, under her breath, as she and the Master stood inspecting the long line of collie benches. "He's having the time of his life! And he's *acting*, too, every minute. I never saw anything so affected!"

Indeed, Wolf was "acting," as frankly and as affectedly as any stagestruck child. Gone was the aloofness he displayed toward strangers at The Place. Standing up in his narrow bench, he surveyed dramatically the passersby and barked in plangent excitement to catch their attention. When anyone stopped to look at him, he would either growl terribly or would make some quite idiotic face or would feign to hunt for a lion in the straw of the bench. Wolf was having a beautiful time.

But the good time was all his. Neither the Mistress nor the Master relished the glances of polite disgust leveled at the poor non-show dog, in this resort of high-quality collies. It made the Mistress unhappy to see fellow-experts eye her dear dog with wondering scorn. It made the Master unreasonably angry. He had planned to say to questioners:

"Oh, this is just a pet collie of ours; not one of our show dogs. We know he hasn't a single good point. We just brought him along for a try at the oldest-and-best-cared-for special."

But when Colonel Rothe anchored his all-conquering Champion Hector of Pogis in the adjoining stall and asked pityingly if Wolf were "all collie or a crossbreed," the Master forgot his own good resolves and snarled back at the inquirer:

"Yes, he's all collie. There's no purer blood in the studbook records. And if you want me to swap him for that freak British importation of yours, you'll have to give me a thousand dollars to boot."

Colonel Rothe was far above bandying words with so churlishly ungracious a neighbor. Favoring poor Wolf with another stare of contemptuous pity, the colonel turned his back on him and began to give careful instructions to his kennelman as to the grooming of the peerless Hector of Pogis.

Rothe was in too good a humor to-day to let the Master's boorishness annoy him. He had surveyed the collies. None there could hope to equal Hector. The garish two-hundred-dollar silver bowl was as good as won by him, before the judging began. The colonel's heart warmed afresh toward his crony and clubmate, Darius Madden, donor of the bowl.

Other collie exhibitors were talking of the luckless Wolf, among themselves, with a charming candor; and were expressing joyously frank opinions of the Mistress and the Master for bringing him to a show. The favorite pastime of too many such exhibitors is a virulent criticism of one another and of one another's dogs. The collie is the cleanest and most sportsmanly dog alive. It seems strange that more professional breeders do not copy his traits.

But now the Mistress came back from a stroll of the collie benches; and with a look of keen distress on her face. Beckoning to her husband she led him along the line; and halted presently in front of another bench.

On this bench lay wearily a magnificent old sable collie. He was all but toothless; fat with the pitiful weight of years; his bleared eyes patient with the sadly hopeless patience of the aged; his muzzle blunted and silvered by age.

"Look!" said the Mistress. "The catalog says he's fifteen years old. I've just been talking with the woman who owns him. She says he was a great showdog, in his prime, and that she hasn't exhibited him in nine years. She brought him along to-day to compete for the cup for oldest-and-best-cared-for collie."

"Well, what of that?" asked the Master, puzzled by her unhappiness. "Wolf will win it away from him. This dog has no teeth and he's half blind and hog fat. Wolf will win the cup, over him, on sheer condition. Don't worry."

"It isn't that," she urged. Don't you see? How can we lead Wolfie —gay, healthy, strong Wolfie—into the ring against this poor old fellow? Why I'd sooner enter a spelling-contest with a deaf-mute! Just look at the dear old chap's dim eyes and that majestic pathos of his! He looks like—like—a dying king. If I should let Wolfie compete against him I'd feel as if I were kicking a—"

"I see!" grumbled the Master, his eyes on the ancient dog. "I see. And the worst part of it is that you're right. As you have a way of being. You're right. We can't show against him. Our trip up here is all for nothing. We'll show Wolf in the Novice Class and in nothing else. I think there are only four collies in the Novice Class. That means he may get fourth prize there. A white ribbon that means nothing. That'll be the net result of our day. Except that Wolf is having a gorgeous time. The rules don't force us to show him for any of the special prizes. And we're not going to compete against this 'dying king.' You're right about that. He looks too much as old Laddie did, at the last. Even *I* would have seen that, in another minute, if you hadn't said anything about it. Well—Wolf is happy. And probably the judge is. The judge who specializes in Chihuahuas and collies! Nobody else seems to be especially merry."

The Master was mistaken in his guess about the judge's happiness. Byron Deene was anything but happy. A month earlier it had seemed to him a simple thing to judge collies as well as his own chosen breed. But as time had gone on, he had lost some of the glow of early enthusiasm; and had forced himself to face the fact that his ignorance of the finer points of a show-collie was abysmal. Now that it was too late to back out, he was honest enough to confess to himself that he was wholly unfit to pass a verdict on collies. But he was not honest enough to confess it to anyone else; and thus to smear his prestige.

Thus, he did, to-day, what has been done too often before and since.

He smuggled to Greenwold, in his pocket, three pages from a marked official catalog of the latest Westminster Show at Madison Square Garden—the pages pertaining to the collie awards. Arriving at Greenwold early, he did what no judge is supposed to do. He bought a catalog of the day's show. Then, with this catalog and the Westminster collie pages, he retired to a secluded corner of the grounds and began to pore over the two documents as carefully as though he were preparing a legal brief.

Several collies at to-day's show had also shown at Westminster. Deene noted how the specialty judge had "placed" them, there, and he memorized their comparative placements. He saw that Champion

Hector of Pogis, for example, had gotten Winners and then Best of Breed, at Westminster. Champion Hector of Pogis was entered for the Greenwold show. The entry read, "For Specials Only." In other words, Hector was not competing for mere points; but for the "special" silver bowl for "Best Collie."

That was good enough for Byron Deene. He could make no mistake in awarding to Hector the special ribbon and silver bowl for Best of Breed; after the regular classes should have been judged. It was very simple. Deene's spirits rose. With meticulous care, he memorized the tag-numbers assigned to to-day's various dogs which had also been shown at Westminster. Most carefully of all did he memorize from the Greenwold catalog the number of Champion Hector of Pogis.

Hector's number, at Greenwold, was 367.

The judge's plan was childlike in its simplicity. Nor, as I have said, was it new. As each dog enters a show ring its owner or handler tells his exhibit's number to the ring steward. The steward thereupon affixes to the exhibitor's arm a huge cardboard slab, bearing in almost equally large figures the dog's number.

Thus, ringside spectators, by help of their catalogs, may follow the judging intelligently—or as nearly intelligently as the average dogshow spectator can be expected to. Thus, also, a judge who had resorted to an unsportsmanly peep at the catalog and whose memory is fairly good, can tell by a covert glance at the exhibitors' arms just which dog is which.

Few judges do this; preferring to make their own decisions, regardless of a dog's record or fame. But it has been done. And to-day Byron Deene sought it as the one certain way out of his dilemma.

Yet, for all his numerical preparation, the judge was increasingly nervous. The ringside crowds confused him. So did the fact that a collie is not judged in the same fashion as is a Chihuahua. From watching idly the judging of collies at one or two long ago shows, Deene had a general idea of such a judge's routine duties;—the ordering of the initial parade of each class, the singling of dog after dog for eye-

and-finger inspection on the block, etc. For the actual deciding between the merits of the dogs he relied on luck and on the numbers he had committed to memory.

Despite all this, he went into the collie ring at the appointed time with dry tongue and wet palms and hot temples and cold feet. Over and over, in his mind, he repeated the numbers he had conned; and their relation to one another. For judging such dogs as had not been mentioned in the Westminster catalog, he must rely on good fortune. And, foremost of all, his mind dwelt on the mystic number, 367; the number of Champion Hector of Pogis, the predestined "Best of Breed."

Deene, had forgotten, of course, what classes Hector or any others might be entered for. There was no need to burden his dizzy brain with any excess information. Enough that he remembered the numbers and the dogs to which those numbers belonged.

First, as usual, came the male classes. First of these was the Puppy Class, the division for all dogs under a year old. Here were but three entrants. One of the trio chanced to have been in the Westminster show. Deene gave him the blue ribbon and took a chance in placing the others in their respective ranks as second and third. As both these others were of mediocre type and with little difference of merit between them, Deene's triple verdict in the Puppy Class was greeted by a murmur of approval from the spectators. Apparently, this unknown judge knew his work and knew it well.

Then came the Novice Class; with five entrants—a mixed lot, except for the winner of the Puppy Class. The Mistress led Wolf into the ring. Or rather, he led her; for he tugged gayly at the leash and pranced and filled the air with clamorous barking; he who as a rule barked only to give an alarm. Through the multiple clangor, she made shift to answer the ring steward's question as to her dog's number. The steward slipped the large-figured pasteboard slab over her arm. The judge stood beside his corner table, watching with apparent dearth of interest this apportioning of the numbers.

Her soft hand chafed by Wolf's excited tugging at the leash, the Mistress on inspiration removed collar and leash from her dog. She knew he could not hope to win anything on points. But by his vehement eagerness to "show" and by his ring manners, he might cajole the judge's amused interest and get the fourth-prize ("reserve") white ribbon, instead of finishing as the prizeless fifth in this class of five dogs.

Wherefore, whispering "Trail!" she kept the boundingly eager collie close at her side, throughout the initial "parade"; without so much as touching him. Similarly, at the call to the central judging block, a word from her sent Wolf bounding over to the block and atop it. There he stood, keyed up to thrilled attention; showing gloriously—if he only had had something to show.

With mechanical quickness Byron Deene examined all five dogs in turn. Then he turned to the table where lay his judging book and its heap of ribbons. Before going near any of the other exhibitors, he crossed to the Mistress, glanced at the number on the pasteboard brassard, noted it down in his book and held out something to her.

The "something" he held out was the dark blue First Prize ribbon of the Novice Class!

He awarded the second ribbon, (the "red,") to the Westminster puppy; and gave out the two other scraps of silk at random to two of the three other dogs in the class.

The Mistress, her face a blank, left the ring with the victoriously frisking Wolf; to confront the Master who stood gaping foolishly at the collie and at the blue ribbon. The ringsiders had murmured again, as the award was given. But this time the murmur was of crass amaze. The thing didn't make sense.

For once, in the history of dogshows, no on-looking collie owner could find immediate breath wherein to indulge the yearning to say something rotten and unsportsmanly about a fellow-exhibitor's dog.

"What in blue blazes!" sputtered the Master, blitheringly, as Wolf danced up to him, followed by the Mistress. "What do you make of it? I've been studying collies for years. And if Wolf is a showdog, then all my study has gone for nothing. Deene actually put him over that splendid tricolor puppy we saw last winter at Madison Square Garden. It—it's—We'll wake up, presently!"

The Mistress, in a daze, was grooming the delighted Wolf with a dandy-brush; while the dog wriggled ecstatically as his psychic brain sensed the bewildered excitement of those around him.

"Here," said the Master, taking the brush from his wife, "I'll do that, for you. But why groom him, now that his class is judged? He—"

"Because he'll have to go into the Winners Class, of course," she replied. "Don't the rules say that the winner of every class must enter the Winners Class?"

"So—why, so they do!" mumbled the Master, coming out of his daze. "Well, that is where Wolf will be snowed under. I wonder if the gorgeous way he 'showed' had anything to do with his victory. Some judges seem to give prizes to a second-rate dog that shows well, over a first-rate dog that won't show. But Wolf isn't even a second-rater. No matter how he shows, in the Winners Class, he'll never get a look-in."

"He's got an AKC blue ribbon, anyhow," boasted the Mistress, happily, "and in good competition, too."

Meantime, the other classes for males—Americanbred, Limit, and the Open events—were judged. By following his carefully memorized numbering and by wiping his dazed mind clear of everything but those numbers and their relative importance, Byron Deene made few errors. None gross enough to call for dismay.

Champion Hector of Pogis, as I have said, was entered "for specials only." That meant he was not called on to compete in any of the regular classes; but must meet the male and the female winner of those classes in the ring, when the Best of Breed (or Best Collie) special should be judged. To the winner of this supreme contest would go the Darius Madden bowl and the kudos thereof.

All dogs, entered for specials only, must make nominal entry in some open class; but need not compete therein. Hector was entered, thus, for Open, Any Color. But he was not one of the four dogs who contested that always-grueling event.

Into the ring came the winners of each of the male "regular classes"; while Rothe and his kennelman stood far to one side grooming Hector for the Big Scene which was to follow as soon as this class should be judged and the female "regular classes" which were to follow it. There were few females. That meant the special for Best of Breed would come up for decision within half an hour. Busily the Colonel and his man wrought over their grand dog.

Four class-winners filed into the ring for the Winners class; Wolf among them. The Mistress, completely flustered by the impossible result of the Novice contest, had forgotten to remove her pasteboard brassard; as do two exhibitors out of three. Coming into the ring with Wolf, now, she still wore it. Two other exhibitors had neglected to remove theirs. The steward handed the fourth his numbered placard.

Again the Mistress unsnapped Wolf's leash and let him go free. Again, at her whispered word, the excited little collie kept close to her during the parade; varying his walk by frequent skipping "grace note" steps, by way of testifying to his delight at this alluring new game. Then as the parade ended, the Mistress came to a halt in a far corner with him; certain there would be no further need for him to show.

She was mistaken.

After an eagle glance at the three other contestants, Deene beckoned her to bring Wolf to the block. Dully ashamed that her dear dog should be singled out in this way as dead wood to be examined and put out of the running before the rest of his class were judged, she obeyed. At a word from the Mistress the collie darted forward and took his place on the platform; striking a gayly tense attitude. Wolf was having a heavenly time, here in the center of the stage and with a thousand eyes on him.

Deene ignored two of the three other entrants and summoned the puppy winner to the block alongside Wolf. From a show-viewpoint there was pitiful difference between the two dogs as they stood there. The Mistress patted Wolf furtively; to comfort him. But he needed no comforting. Seldom had he been more keenly happy.

Then the judge scribbled two numbers in his book; and handed the Mistress the purple Winner's Rosette; giving the bicolored Reserve Winner ribbon to the puppy's handler.

Amid a deathly silence the bewildered Mistress led Wolf from the ring; and took him across to where the speechless Master was standing.

"This isn't a dream, dear," she said, confusedly. "It's a delirium. We'll both wake presently in a hospital, with pretty ice-packs on our heads. It's—it's impossible!"

The Master was past words. Not a soul came near the two to offer congratulations on the incomprehensible triumph of an elderly non-show dog over the best collies in the Eastern states.

The female classes were in the ring. It was well for Byron Deene that there were few females in the show. For, momentarily, he was waxing more and more rattled and was clinging with ever-greater difficulty to his memorized numbers.

These classes being disposed of in haphazard fashion, the ring was cleared for the judging of the specials. The first special was the two-hundred-dollar silver bowl, for Best of Breed. Into the ring came the winner of the female classes. Into the ring strode Colonel Rothe, with Champion Hector of Pogis marching proudly at his side.

Back on the benches, two dogs had started an impromptu fight. Two hundred other dogs cheered them on with a babel of barks and yelps. Through the tumult, Colonel Rothe shouted his dog's number in reply to the steward's question. The steward went over to the diminished pile of brassards, selected one and placed it obsequiously on the Colonel's pudgy left arm. Rothe smiled in calm anticipation.

Byron Deene looked coldly upon the female winner and then on Champion Hector of Pogis. His eyes sweeping the ringside, he demanded loudly of his steward:

"Where is the male winner?"

The Mistress heard the boomed question. Still in a dumb nightmare she led Wolf into the ring. The little dog danced along, ecstatic at another chance to show off, before all these humans and fellow-collies. To the block he trotted, proudly, not waiting for commands. There he stood, in impudent joy, posturing and posing dramatically for the benefit of an unsympathetic audience.

Judge Byron Deene cut short the performance by scribbling a number in his book, and then handing the Mistress the red-white-and-blue ribbon which symbolized Wolf's title to Best of Breed and his winning of the coveted silver bowl.

The moment's hush of horror was broken by a muffled explosion of profanity which arose simultaneously from opposite sides of the ring;—where stood Colonel Rothe and Darius Madden.

Never was the mystery explained to the two who exulted incredulously over it, nor to the two who swore colorfully over it, nor to the throng who marveled bemusedly at it.

None of them knew that when the low-voiced Mistress had entered the ring for the Novice class and had told the steward her number was "357," the confused man had misunderstood her, through the babel of noise and had given her the brassard numbered "367."

None knew that when Rothe shouted thickly through the racket, demanding his number, the steward had given him "357"—a brassard which had gone unused throughout the show; and which sounded more like "367" than did any other in the heap on the table. The Colonel not only was nearsighted, but, like nine exhibitors out of ten, he had not thought to glance down at his arm to verify the number.

There was nothing new about this mix-up of brassards. Often before and since has it happened. But there was something dynamically new about Wolf's one and only show-victory. The gallant little collie was inordinately proud;—though he did not at all know what had happened.

CHAPTER VII: THE LAST ADVENTURE

CHAPTER VII: THE LAST ADVENTURE

SHE was not a collie. Heaven alone knew what she was. She was nondescript and thin and homely. She belonged to nobody. In fact, she was one of those worthless examples of chance breeding which should never have been permitted to be born, still less to live.

People grate gravely about eugenics among humans—where it never can have a chance to be enforced. People neglect eugenics among dogs—where it can be enforced with entire ease. The result is a swarm of mongrels. Many of these mongrels are beautiful and wise and valuable. Some are not. This particular dog was the least promising of the heterogeneous mongrel clan.

Wolf met her by the merest chance;—a lucky chance for her and a fatal chance for him.

He was lying drowsily in the lakeside summerhouse of The Place, one warm May afternoon, behind the hammock wherein the Mistress and the Master were reading.

Down the lake, from a boys' camp, a mile above, came a boat; with three of the young campers in it. Two of the boys were rowing. A third sat in the stern. He was holding by the neck a most disreputable yellowish gray dog; bone-thin and unkempt.

The dog was collarless. But around her stringy throat was tied a thick rope. To the other end of the rope was tied a stone. The story told itself to the Mistress and her husband, as the boat passed in front of the summerhouse.

"Look!" cried the Mistress, in keen distress. "They're going to drown that poor dog. See the stone and the rope? Oh, *don't* let them!"

"What's the main idea?" called the Master, hailing the boat's occupants.

"This dog's been hanging round our camp," called back the lad in the stern. "She's stole our grub, a couple of times. We stoned her away, but she always comes back. We're going to get rid of her. We didn't want to drown her, up where we swim. It's bad for the water. So we're rowing her down to the dam. Going to throw her over the falls. She —"

"You're going to do nothing of the kind!" blazed the Mistress, jumping up and running to the edge of the lake. "You're not—"

"She ain't your dog, is she?" retorted the boy in the stern; speaking with all the exquisite courtesy which amateur campers are wont to bestow on the luckless householders of the regions they honor with their outings. "Then s'pose you mind your own business; if you've got any business to mind?"

His two companions laughed in glad applause of this chivalric reply. The mongrel, at sound of the Mistress's voice, had gotten to her feet and was whining in anguished appeal.

Too evidently, the poor dog realized the fate in store for her and was pleading frenziedly for aid to this friendly human who had spoken in her behalf.

Wolf had come to the lakeside with the Mistress. And the wise little old collie read the mongrel's whimpered appeal as well as if it were couched in words. He growled; and ran out a few feet into the water.

The Master had departed, on a bee-line for The Place's nearby boathouse. He was traveling rapidly.

It was not on the free list for anyone to speak to the Mistress as the camper in the stern had spoken. The only way to wreak punishment was from another boat.

The youth in the stern noted the man's hurried progress toward the boathouse. Being a lad of action, he did not dream away the intervening moments; but shouted to the two rowers to put on speed. As he gave this order, he proceeded to lighten the boat by heaving the mongrel overboard.

Away sped the oarsmen, upstream, toward the safety of their camp and the loving protection of the scoutmasters. The miserable dog fell into the water with a resounding splash.

The fall carried the mongrel far beneath the surface; the stone dragging her down. But, with amazing lack of efficiency, the boys had affixed to the rope a stone somewhat too light for its lethal purpose.

Under water went the unfortunate mongrel, fighting futilely for life. Her mad battling brought her to the surface for a fleeting space. Then the weight of the stone and her own lack of strength dragged her under, again.

The Mistress waded out from the bank, forgetful of thin slippers and silk stockings. But at the second step, she paused. A more potent rescuer was on the job.

As the mongrel had tumbled into the water, Wolf had dashed after her. Now, swimming with a force which carried his shoulders high above the level, he was forging forward to where she had vanished.

There was a feeble swirl, just ahead. And again the mongrel's nose appeared, briefly. By a last despairing effort of puny strength, she had managed to counteract the weight of the stone, once more, and to battle her way back from the weedy depths.

But it was very apparently a last effort; and a feeble one at that. For, as soon as her head appeared it began to go under again.

The boat had been scarcely a hundred feet offshore when the boy tossed her overboard. And that hundred feet of space had been covered swiftly by Wolf's race through the ripples.

Now, as the mongrel began to sink, Wolf's strong jaws caught her by the nape of the neck. Churning the waters in his struggle to bear up the double weight of dog and stone, he spun about and made for shore; his white forepaws smiting the water to foam, his white teeth fixed as lightly in his exhausted burden's neck as the strain of upholding her would permit.

It was a gallant piece of work; and it called for all his compact strength. Snail-like was his shoreward progress. More than once the weak writhings of the mongrel submerged his head as well as hers.

But ever he fought on. And this was Wolf's way. Not from birth to death did he understand the meaning of defeat or of drawing back from anything he had begun.

The rescuer and the rescued were halfway to shore when the Master came rowing around the point of land between the summerhouse and the boathouse. A call from his wife, ankle-deep in water, directed his attention from the already far-distant boys to the two half-drowned dogs.

He rowed over to them. With his fingers hooked in Wolf's collar, he sought to lift the collie into the careening boat. But, as if divining his purpose and aware of what must befall the helplessly wornout mongrel if she were let go, Wolf held his tight grip on the scruff of her neck.

Confronted with this double burden, the Master knelt down in the bottom of the boat, bracing himself and seeking to trim the leaky craft for the impending heave.

Wolf looked up steadfastly and even gayly into the Master's face; happily confident that his own tough work was over and that his god would take over the tiresome job.

With some difficulty, the man lifted the two dogs over the gunwale and into the boat; shipping several gallons of lake water as he did so. Water that swished merrily about the knees and legs of his white flannel trousers and soaked him to the skin.

Wolf relaxed his grasp on the mongrel as soon as the latter was safe. Then, standing up, he proceeded to shake himself, rapidly and with much thoroughness; the spray from his rough gold-red coat deluging the Master afresh.

But the mongrel did not get up. She made no attempt to move. Slumpingly inert, she lay sprawled in the bottom of the boat, panting loudly; her eyes shut, the water streaming from her sparse coat and from her loosely open jaws. She was nearer dead than alive.

A homeless existence and such scanty food as can be cadged from rural ashcans and occasional camp garbage-heaps—these do not conduce to strength in a dog. The fright and shock had completed her utter collapse.

She lay, moveless, when the Master landed on the bank beside the summerhouse. Wolf on the contrary hopped gleefully ashore, and once more treated his drenched coat to a very thorough shaking—this time over much of the Mistress's white organdie dress.

"In all my days," grumbled the Master, staring morbidly down at his own wrecked costume, "I never yet went out of my way to do a decent thing without having reason afterward to be sorry I did it. My clothes look like the last hours of a misspent life. And all to save a mutt that is better dead! . . . I suppose that boatload of brats is too far away, by this time, for me to overhaul it and capsize them. Wolf, if you hadn't saved what wasn't worth saving, we'd all be better off."

Wolf grinned and wagged his short bushy tail vigorously, at sound of his name. Then he trotted back to where the panting mongrel sprawled. He bent over her, licking her face and seeming to urge her to rise.

She opened her bleared eyes and wagged her lank tail weakly. But she made no effort to get up. Her cowed gaze drifted to the two humans. There was hopeless pathos in the look.

"That settles it!" growled the Master, forestalling his wife's plea. "We're saddled with her. The fact that she's weak and worthless is enough to make you champion her. All right. I'll carry her up to the barn and give her some aromatic. When she's able to get onto her feet again, a square meal will complete her cure."

Thus it was that a mongrel came to that home of thoroughbred collies. Nobody could be found to claim her. So she remained at The Place. The Mistress named her "Undine," because she had risen from the waters.

Undine was a meek and gentle and timorous creature. Gratefully and cringingly she rewarded the care lavished on her. For the first time in her life she was receiving food instead of fright; care instead of kicks. She throve on the new treatment. Unobtrusive, gladly content to sleep in the barn and to confine her wanderings to the stable yard and the vegetable garden, she was little trouble to anyone.

The astonishing change from starvation to good fare made her into another animal. In less than a month, her scraggy body was rounding out into lines of comparative grace. Health, and an occasional brushing from the Mistress, gave her coat a certain luster and growth. Always she would remain a mongrel. Always she would remain cowed and stupid and homely. But she was no longer a scarecrow.

Wolf constituted himself her staunch protector and chum. He was strangely human in many ways. It is a human trait, for instance, to care more for those whom we have helped than for those who have helped us. And this trait was strong in Wolf. Always he seemed to remember he had saved Undine from death; and the deed appeared to bind him to her for any future services.

He would forsake his big collie chum, Bobby, for a ramble with the homely mongrel who rewarded his friendliness with slavish adoration. He would fly furiously at any of the other thoroughbred collies of The Place that resented with snarl or growl the presence of the plebeian Undine among them.

The average collie has reduced snobbishness to a fine art. These purebred prizewinning dogs looked on Undine as a lowbred interloper. But for Wolf's fiery championship, her life with them would have been scarcely more bearable than had been her olden tramplike career.

Yet she was beautifully happy. And she treated her rescuer with flattering worship. Her stormtossed life-bark had drifted into a mighty pleasant harbor. She reveled in the fullfed comfort of The Place.

The Mistress and the Master viewed with secret amusement this new friendship of their little old chum, Wolf. Very dear had Wolf become to them both, in these past few years.

Not only was he the acknowledged king of The Place's dogs; but he was the chief house-comrade of his two human deities. His place in the dining room was on the floor beside the Mistress's chair. He had succeeded to Lad's "cave" beneath the piano. Placidly, happily, advanced age was stealing upon him.

At ten, he had the vigor and fire of a three-year-old. His compactly powerful body had not yet taken on the blur of fat. His big dark eyes were still clear and bright. His teeth were un-yellowed.

Only by a few white hairs in his black eyelashes and by a slight silvering of the muzzle and by an occasional indisposition to romp did he show that Time was beginning to lay a gently heavy hand on him.

Once in a great while, into his face would creep, fleetingly, the unmistakable and infinitely pathetic expression of an old dog. But, for the most part, he showed not an outward sign of age.

Yes, the Indian Summer of his adventurous life had set in. But it had set in benignly and all-but imperceptibly. His days were sunnily happy at The Place; and now that Laddie and Bruce were gone he stood first in the affections of the woman and the man he worshiped.

The early tempest years were past. Chill age had not set in. Wise and contented, he was rounding out happily his span of years. The elfin fun and the dashing gayety were still his. But they were tempered by wisdom.

Generations of collies had come and gone. Wolf remained. He was as much a part of The Place's life as was Fritz, the Master's thirty-three-year-old saddle horse, which had been bred and reared at The Place and which now enjoyed a lazily workless old age, in box-stall and paddock; with daily lumps of sugar and much petting.

It was hard to imagine life at The Place without Wolf's queerly compelling personality as a component part of it.

When at last Undine had waxed sleek and healthy, the Master found a home for her. A farmer who lived some two miles from The Place, on the far side of the railroad tracks, wanted a dog.

He came to The Place to price a collie puppy. But as such a pup was beyond his means he was induced to accept Undine as a gift.

He and his family quickly grew fond of the gentle and timid mongrel. They made a pet of her. Undine's housing problem seemed definitely settled.

But Wolf thought otherwise. So did Undine.

A week after the mongrel had been inducted into her new abode, the Master came downstairs and onto the veranda one morning, to find Wolf and Undine waiting, side by side, on the porch to greet him.

For the past two years, winter and summer, Wolf had slept at night on an old coat, on the couch in the Master's study. Vastly proud was the little collie of his indoor sleeping quarters. The study windows stood open all night, in warm weather.

(A burglar might as safely have stepped on a rattlesnake as to have ventured in through one of those windows, with Wolf on guard inside.)

Occasionally in the early morning, Wolf would jump out through an open window for a stroll of the grounds.

Apparently, he had gone out much earlier than usual, on this particular morning; or else he had sallied forth during the night. Somehow he had found his way to the two-mile distant farmhouse, across the tracks—where never had he been taken and which he had located nobody knew how. His discovery of Undine's new abode was one of the many unexplainable things about Wolf.

Thither had he gone in search of his homesick friend, Undine. He had chewed diligently at the rope with which she was tied to her kennel-coop; and at last he had severed it. Then he had escorted her back to The Place.

Now, with jaws agrin and white feet dancing and tail wildly wagging, he greeted the scowling Master. Wolf was monstrous proud of his nocturnal exploit.

At the Master's mild reproof, he sought to look crestfallen. But the attempt was a failure. Unquestionably, the collie felt a dramatic thrill in his own cleverness in finding and releasing and bringing home again the undesired mongrel.

After breakfast, Wolf was shut up in the study, to his great indignation. The Mistress and the Master motored over to the farm, with the unwilling Undine. There the mongrel was received with joy by the whole family, who had been standing sadly in front of her empty kennel, viewing the chewed rope.

"Better try a chain, next time," advised the Master. "Wolf's teeth are like shears. Besides, he has taught her the trick, now. She'll probably gnaw her own rope in two without his help. Buy a strong chain, instead. Even Wolf can't bite through that."

"I'll do still better," volunteered the farmer. "I've got a roll of chicken wire, left over from fencing my hen-yard. I'll build a wire run around Undine's coop. Then she won't need to be tied up, at all. She'll be comfortabler, anyhow, in a runyard than tugging at a rope. It'll give her more space to move around in."

"So *that's* settled," observed the Master as he and his wife drove homeward. "We've seen the last of the unlovely Undine. Poor old Wolf! He'll miss her."

"If he misses her," said the Mistress with quiet certainty, "he'll find some way to bring her back to The Place. I know Wolfie. What he wants to do, he does."

"Nonsense!" scoffed the Master, with true masculine superiority. "Wolf is pretty clever. But he won't be able to bite a hole in a chicken wire, wide enough to let Undine through. No, thank goodness, we've seen the last of her!"

The Mistress made no reply. Seldom did she argue. Far more seldom was she mistaken in one of her conjectures.

So it was that she felt no surprise at all, next morning, when she and her husband came out on the veranda before breakfast, to find Wolf and the humbly ingratiating Undine awaiting them on the door-mat.

Wolf's white forepaws were brown with new dirt. It had taken him more than an hour to dig a tunnel under the wire runway, and to coax Undine to wriggle out through the hole.

But at last the escape had been achieved. And he and she had gotten clear of the yard before the first member of the early-rising farmer's family was awake.

The Master looked foolishly at the two dogs and then at his wife. The Mistress was busily admonishing Wolf for his share in the prison-breaking; and she gave no sign that she noted her husband's air of ridiculous self-humiliation.

"I'm afraid," she said at last, "I'm afraid he's made up his mind to keep on rescuing her, till the end of the chapter; and leading her back here in triumph. I can't blame him for doing it. She is so fond of him; and he has elected himself her guardian ever since he saved her from drowning. I suppose he thinks he is rescuing her all over again, each time he sets her free."

"What's the use?" demanded the Master, glumly. "I've too much work to do, to spend half an hour every morning, taking the measly cur back to where she belongs. But you're right about his keeping on trying to get her lose. He knows it was a clever stunt. He knows *we* know it. That means he'll keep right on doing it—if he can. That's Wolf, all over."

"If the three children, over there, hadn't gotten so fond of her," said the Mistress, "I'd suggest we keep her here. Then Wolf would be happy; and so would she."

"And when people came here to see the collies," returned the Master, "they'd be sure to see her, first of all; and they'd think she was typical of all the rest of our dogs. No, thanks. Back she goes, the minute breakfast is over. If the man had done as I told him to, she couldn't have gotten loose. I told him to *chain* her, you remember. But of course that would mean he'd have to pay for a chain and a collar. He's a cautious spendthrift. He had the chicken-wire handy; so he tried to save money by using that, instead. I'll tell him that the next time Undine comes sneaking over here, I'll put a bullet through her foolish head. Maybe that'll induce him to get her a collar and a chain."

He spoke with truculence. As usual, the Mistress read him correctly.

"You couldn't be hired to shoot her," she challenged, laughing. "You know perfectly well you couldn't."

"I didn't say I could," the Master defended himself, sulkily. "I said that's what I'd *tell* him. And I shall. Let's go to breakfast, shan't we? Come along, Wolf."

Leaving Undine to wait for him on the mat, Wolf followed the two humans into the sunny breakfast room. There, as usual, he lay beside the Mistress's chair.

There, as usual, he received from her a fragment of buttered toast. Thence, presently—timing it to a fraction of a second—he went to the other end of the table, just as the Master laid down his egg-spoon.

For years it had been Wolf's custom to cross over to the Master, at that precise moment of the morning meal; to receive from him the emptied egg cup and to lap therefrom such few particles as might still adhere to its sides.

Never by the wink of an eye did Wolf fail to reach the Master's chair just as the spoon was laid down.

Even when the dog chanced to have been lying with his back to the Master he calculated the time to perfection; though nobody could figure how he did it. It was one of the scores of things about Wolf that no human could explain.

Breakfast over, the collie was shut once more, ignominously, into the study, while the Mistress and the Master took Undine to the farmhouse. As a rule, Wolf loved the study. He loved it as his dead chum, the golden champion, Sigurd, ("Treve") had loved it. Most of all, he loved the disreputable old couch on one corner of which was the ragged tweed coat which was his bed.

But it was one thing to enter the study from choice; and quite another thing to be shut in. Wherefore, nose between paws, Wolf lay in gloomy brooding; until his acute ears detected, a mile away, the hum of The Place's car. Hundreds of cars passed along that road, every day. Yet out of them all, Wolf could distinguish the purr of that one motor.

He got up and trotted to the study door; his sulks forgotten. Five minutes later, the returning Master opened the door and let him out.

"Well, old friend," observed the Master, "he has promised me to go over to the village, before noon, and get a chain for the unspeakable Undine. You'll wear your teeth out, before you can scissor a chain in two. Best stay at home. It's none too safe for you to be crossing the railroad tracks, every time you come and go between there and The Place. Just forget Undine. She isn't worth remembering. I'm afraid you've got low tastes, Wolf."

"He's too wise to get into trouble from trains," said the Mistress, in the hallway behind her husband. "Wolf has a wholesome respect for trains. I suppose he got it, years ago, from seeing us slow the car when we come to a track, and look up and down. Anyway, that's just what he does, whenever we're out walking and cross a railroad track. He knows more than most people, about avoiding trains and automobiles. . . . He knows more about *everything*, than most people. Don't you, Wolfie, you queer little dog?"

Wolf wagged his tail, and wiggled affectedly, at the sound of his name and at the note of praise in her voice. Then, falling in at her heels as usual, he followed her and the Master out onto the porch.

The day was hot and breathless; the kind of day which, in the hill country of northern New Jersey, is almost certain to be followed by a thunderstorm. On the driveway three or four young collie puppies were at play.

Wolf was about to curl himself up at the Mistress's feet as she sat down to read her mail, when he wheeled about; his ear caught by a familiar sound.

A big delivery truck was turning in at the gate, a furlong above; and was starting down the woodland driveway at carelessly high speed. The collie puppies continued to frisk about in the drive, heedless of the approaching menace.

Like a red-gold flash, Wolf was off the veranda and springing out among them. For perhaps the thousandth time in his ten years of life he was herding thoughtless dogs out of harm's way and to the safety of the driveside turf.

So fast did the truck approach, to-day, that he barely had time to shoulder the last of the puppies out of danger before it was on him.

With entire ease, despite his growing weight of years, Wolf dodged aside from under the grinding wheels of the vehicle as its driver put on all his brakes. Then the collie, as always, came mincing back to the Mistress, to be praised for this bit of swift herding.

"One of these days," prophesied the Master, irately, "Wolf is going to get killed, that way. Sometime, he is going to miscalculate the distance; and get hit by a car. He takes chances that get on my nerves."

"No automobile is ever going to kill Wolfie," contradicted the Mistress, serenely confident of her pet's ability to protect himself. "He's too wise."

As usual, the Master's prophecy was wrong; while, as usual, hers was correct.

That evening, Wolf was left on the veranda, while the Mistress and the Master went to a dinner a few miles away. The collie did not consider himself to be on guard. It was far too early in the night for that.

Besides, his chum, big auburn-and-white Bobby, was lying on the porch, near him; to serve as watchdog, if need should arise.

Wolf wearied of the tedium of waiting for the return of the two humans. His thoughts went to Undine and to the encored jolly adventure of freeing her from captivity.

On the two former times he had not set forth to the farm until long after midnight; when he had chanced to wake from his snooze on the study couch. But there seemed no good reason, on this lonely evening, to postpone his trip to such an hour or to let it break in on his night's rest.

He got to his feet in leisurely fashion, stretched himself fore-and-aft; yawned; and started up the driveway at an unhurried trot.

Out into the highroad he trotted, heading for the farm. He kept to one side of the thoroughfare; giving room to any and all motor cars.

The Mistress had been right in saying that motors were no menace to Wolf. By uncanny wisdom and long experience he could thread his way through a jumble of them, without hurt.

Across the lake bridge he went. Then, leaving the road, he cut acrosslots. Another half mile brought him to the railroad tracks. As always, he slackened speed just before he reached the rails; and glanced up and down the right-of-way.

On the stoops of trackside cottages lounged several tired workers. To these Wolf gave no heed, as he passed on. Humans—apart from the Mistress and the Master—had never interested him.

Then he was in the farmhouse yard. A light or two still burned in the house itself; for ten o'clock had not struck. A whimper of eager friendliness from somewhere to the rear of the yard welcomed the collie. Silent as was his padding advance, Undine had heard and scented him.

Wolf trotted to her kennel, and he and she touched noses in greeting. Wolf was dancingly elated at the bit of mischief he had planned. To him it seemed a rare joke to outwit Undine's new owner by setting her free from her clumsy bond-age, every night; and taking her back to The Place.

He could read human faces and human voices—yes and human emotions—with eerie skill. And from this power he knew that neither the Mistress nor the Master had been really angered at his releasing of Undine.

He knew that it had amused them both, in spite of the Master's grumblings; and that they considered it clever. Wherefore, Wolf was minded to repeat the exploit as often and as long as it should continue to make a hit. Which is not only dog nature, but human nature.

But to-night, on his very first glance at the tied mongrel, Wolf saw his task promised new difficulties. For the tie-rope was replaced by a rusty length of chain.

The farmer had saved the cost of a new chain by hunting around in the stored rubbish of his barn loft until he came upon this ancient string of rust-scored links. With it he had fastened Undine to the kennel.

Decrepit as was the chain, it was still too strong for Undine to break it, by the most energetic jerk. Also, it was proof against gnawing. Wolf had sense enough to know this, without trying. And, according to his custom, he wasted no time in vain efforts at achieving the impossible.

Finding the chain unbreakable and unbitable, he nosed at Undine's neck. Here again the "cautious spendthrift" had saved money. Instead of buying a collar, he had made one out of rope; slipping a chain-ring through it, by which to fasten the dog.

This knowledge was quite enough for Wolf. While Undine stood stockstill, the collie's sharp white incisor-teeth wrought scientifically at the thick rope collar. The rope, though stout of appearance, was long past its first toughness. Like most things on the farm, it was on the decline.

The task of severing it was simple. In a few minutes the rusting chain clanked dully to the ground. Undine frisked out into the yard, collarless and free.

She was very happy. Not only had her adored protector set her at liberty again, but she was going back with him to The Place and away from this mean abode where she was so homesick. Her wonted cringing meekness gave place to a coweringly frolicsome mood.

Without waiting for Wolf to lead the way, she scampered out of the yard and over the fields, heading for The Place and traveling at a shambling gallop.

Wolf followed at a trot—the deceptively fast and choppy wolf-trot of a collie; which eats up the distance almost as rapidly as does any other dog's canter.

Gradually, Undine's first elated gallop was slowing down. Wolf was only a few yards behind her as the two moved past the group of trackside cottages with the handful of workers still lounging on the stoops.

Idly these folk glanced at the dogs as the two chanced to cross the bars of light from the windows. But—at first—the humans took no heed of the runaways.

The night was sick-hot. The cottagers' eyes strayed with tired interest to the thunderstorm piling up from the northwest—the storm that might break the hot spell; and whose saffron flares of heat-lightning were staining the fat black cloud-rack almost continuously.

Then came a more distinct sound than the stifled groan of far-off thunder; and a clearer gleam than the cloud-hidden lightning could boast.

From around the curve echoed the warning whistle-note and rumble of the oncoming Stroudsburg Express—ten minutes late and making up lost time. The glow of the unseen headlight cast a flicker of diffused radiance through the night.

Undine's gallop had slowed to a trot. Now she became aware of a pestilentially biting flea supping behind her left ear. The flea bit deep into the tender flesh. Undine prepared to rid herself of him.

Halting, she sat down, and began to scratch her left ear vehemently with her left hind-claws.

Wolf had caught up to her, just as she began these scratching-operations against the flea. He too had come to a standstill. For he had heard the train and had seen its glow.

As ever, he stopped and looked up and down the track. The train had not yet appeared around the nearby bend. So he crossed the track and glanced back to see what was delaying Undine.

There sat the misfortune-breeding mongrel, scratching luxuriously at her ear; oblivious to everything but the joy of abating the flea.

She was sitting in the precise center of the track, midway between the two humming rails.

Wolf barked a sharp warning. Undine did not so much as turn her head at his summons. Stupid, her narrow-gauge brain wholly occupied with the flea, she was oblivious of all else.

Around the curve roared the Stroudsburg Express. Its headlight hurled a blinding white glare along the tracks. The loungers on the stoops beheld Undine, scratching away, directly in its path.

Now the flood of dazzling light made her look up stupidly from her labors. Directly above her towered the bulk of the locomotive. She was engulfed in a sea of hideous brilliancy.

Scared past all powers of motion or of thought, she cowered shivering between the rails.

Then it was that Wolf did what he had been training, all his life to do. The mighty heart of old Lad, his sire, ran true to form in this wise little son of his.

Wolf had a painfully clear knowledge of the dangers that lurk on a railroad track. He had known of them, not only by instinct and from the Mistress's repeated warnings, but from awful memory of seeing a dog cut in two by a train, years earlier.

Yes, Wolf knew the peril. He knew the certain and dread price he must pay for what he was going to do. Wolf was anything but a fool.

Gayly he whizzed forward; a bark of joyous challenge ripping through the thunder of the train. To his death he dashed; as to a romp.

The loungers saw a flash of ruddy-gold-and-white dart into the glare of the track. They saw Wolf snatch Undine by the back, between his mighty jaws. They saw him swing her bodily into the air. They saw him sling her free of the rails.

It was all done in the flicker of an eyelash—almost faster than the human eye could follow—there in front of the on-rushing locomotive.

Undine, screeching in helpless terror, hurtled through the air and rolled unhurt down the cinder-packed embankment to the safety of the shallow ditch.

Wolf, in practically the same motion, sprang back; with the lightning swiftness of a tiger cat. To within the merest hairsbreadth of space, he gauged his distance aright.

The grinding wheels missed him. So did the bulk of the locomotive. A bit of outjutting metalwork, at one corner of the cow-catcher, touched him on the side of the skull. That was all.

When the unheeding train had raged past, leaving dust-eddies and a new blackness in its singing wake, the folk from the cottages came out with flashlights. They found Undine whining and sniffing above something at the trackside.

His red-gold coat unruffled, his beautiful body stretched out lazily as if for slumber, and without one disfiguring mark on it, lay Wolf.

Over him whimpered dazedly the mongrel;—the useless cur for which the hero collie had so blithely tossed away his vivid life.

"And yet," commented an editorial, a few days later, when a hundred newspapers all over America had told the tale of Wolf's shining death, "and yet people speak contemptuously of 'dying like a dog!' "

THE END